C900067

D1141401

Wildfire Island Docs

Welcome to Paradise!

Meet the small but dedicated team of medics
who service the remote Pacific Wildfire Island.

In this idyllic setting relationships are rekindled,
passions are stirred, and bonds that will last a
lifetime are forged in the tropical heat…

But there's also a darker side to paradise—secrets,
lies and greed amidst the Lockhart family threaten
the community, and the team find themselves fighting
to save more than the lives of their patients. They
must band together to fight for the future of the island
they've all come to call home!

Read Caroline and Keanu's story in
The Man She Could Never Forget
by Meredith Webber

Read Anna and Luke's story in
The Nurse Who Stole His Heart
by Alison Roberts

Read Maddie and Josh's story in
Saving Maddie's Baby
by Marion Lennox

Read Sarah and Harry's story in
A Sheikh to Capture Her Heart
by Meredith Webber

All available now!

Dear Reader,

The very best thing about writing this book was that I shared the experience with two very good friends. Together we set up Wildfire Island, and over a couple of years we got together to refine the stories and make them work together.

Recently Marion Lennox, from Victoria, Alison Roberts, from New Zealand, and I were on the Gold Coast in Queensland, where I live. They'd rented a lovely apartment high on a hill above the beach, from where they could look out at the whales passing south after the annual pilgrimage to our shores. Together we sat watching the stunning views and talked about our characters, who were very real people to us by then, and we sorted out the very last chapter of the last book so all our readers would know what had happened to everyone a year or so later.

Such fun! We hadn't done a series together since Crocodile Creek, and it was a great challenge to have.

All the best,

Meredith Webber

A SHEIKH
TO CAPTURE
HER HEART

BY
MEREDITH WEBBER

Published in Great Britain 2016
By Mills & Boon, an imprint of HarperCollins*Publishers*
1 London Bridge Street, London, SE1 9GF

© 2016 Meredith Webber

ISBN: 978-0-263-26387-9

Our policy is to use papers that are natural, renewable and recyclable products and made from wood grown in sustainable forests. The logging and manufacturing processes conform to the legal environmental regulations of the country of origin.

Printed and bound in Great Britain
by CPI Antony Rowe, Chippenham, Wiltshire

Meredith Webber lives on the sunny Gold Coast in Queensland, Australia, but takes regular trips west into the Outback, fossicking for gold or opals. These breaks in the beautiful and sometimes cruel red earth country provide her with an escape from the writing desk and a chance for the mind to roam free—not to mention getting some much needed exercise. They also supply the kernels of so many stories it's hard for her to stop writing!

Books by Meredith Webber

Mills & Boon Medical Romance

Taming Dr Tempest
Melting the Argentine Doctor's Heart
Orphan Under the Christmas Tree
New Doc in Town
The Sheikh and the Surrogate Mum
Christmas Where She Belongs
One Baby Step at a Time
Date with a Surgeon Prince
The Accidental Daddy
The Sheikh Doctor's Bride
The One Man to Heal Her

Visit the Author Profile page
at millsandboon.co.uk for more titles.

To all my writing friends,
but in particular Marion and Alison.

CHAPTER ONE

RAHMAN AL-TARAQ WAS BROODING. At least, that was what he assumed he was doing, but, never having been what he'd consider a moody man, it had taken a while to reach that conclusion.

If asked, he'd have described himself as a—well, *driven* was probably the only word—man. Driven to succeed, to prove himself, to be the best he could and garner admiration for his achievements rather than for having, purely by chance, been born into royalty.

Wealthy royalty!

It wasn't that the servants at the palace where he'd grown up had bowed and scraped, but very early on he'd realised that every whim would be granted and treats of all kinds supplied, not because he'd done something to deserve them but because of who he was.

What other six-year-old boy would be given an elephant for his birthday, simply because he'd happened to mention in passing that the elephant he'd seen in a travelling show shouldn't have to live with a chain around its foot?

That thought made him smile!

Imagine bringing Rajah here, to this tropical paradise in the South Pacific! He'd love the rainforest, but would decimate the villagers' gardens in a week.

Maybe less.

Besides which he was getting too old to travel.

He sighed, a sure sign he was brooding, and as brooding was a totally pointless occupation and achieved precisely nothing, a man who was into achievement—or had been—should do something about it.

He stood up and paced the bure he'd had built for himself as part of his exclusive resort on Wildfire Island, his eyes barely registering the beauty of the natural stone, the polished, ecologically sourced timber, the intricately woven local mats. From outside it might look like a typical island home, but inside…

In truth, he might be driven to achieve recognition for his work, but he didn't mind a few trappings of luxury.

Work!

There was that word again.

No matter how hard he tried to convince himself the work he was doing now was important and worthwhile, which it was, there was always a but.

His drive to be himself apart from his background had begun as a child sent to England at ten to a top boarding school. On arrival he'd introduced himself as Harry so his more exotic name didn't mark him out.

And as Harry, he'd been driven to succeed, to be the best, and his rise through school and university had been marked with success. But he'd found his true passion to be for surgery—general at first then specialising in paediatric surgery, helping save the lives of the most vulnerable small humans.

But one could hardly operate on a newborn with a

right hand that trembled, legacy of a touch-and-go brush with encephalitis. His initial reaction to the loss of the work he loved had been fury—fury with the weakness of his body in doing this to him.

Eventually he'd realised the pointlessness of his anger, so he'd sought and found a new focus—to provide facilities for scientists working on a variety of vaccines for the disease, as well as developing mosquito eradication programmes in the worst affected areas.

It was worthwhile work, and it had him roaming the world almost continually, checking up on the services he'd set up. Which left him tired. But it didn't become the passion his surgical work had been, and he felt a lesser man because of it.

He sighed and went back to brooding, but on the woman this time—better, surely, than brooding on the past and the loss of the work he'd loved.

What was done was done!

The woman!

Sarah Watson...

He *had* met her before, he was certain of that.

But having come close to death from the encephalitis virus had obviously killed some brain cells and though his memory of her was vivid in his mind, he couldn't place it in context anywhere.

He'd asked her at the cocktail party, caught up with her in the crush at the opening of the refurbished research station and resort, reminded her they'd met.

And she'd denied it—brushed away from him—telltale colour in her cheeks suggesting it was a lie.

But why?

And why in damnation did he care?

Worse, care enough to have returned to the island

in order to see her again when he could have been in Africa, or, if he really needed a woman, in New York, where there were beautiful, fun, sophisticated women who wanted nothing more than a brief sexual relationship with no strings attached?

It was her hair!

How many women had hair the colour of rich, polished mahogany?

And the scent of it—tangy—like vinegar mixed with the rose perfume his mother always wore, and the rose-scented water that splashed in the fountains at home.

But vinegar?

Could he really have picked up vinegar in the scent—*and* been drawn to it?

Who was drawn to vinegar?

Whatever!

The fact remained he *had* to have brushed against her some time in the past, for the scent to have been so evocative as they'd passed in the crush of people at the cocktail party! He'd asked his friend Luke about the woman and had learnt nothing more than that she was the general surgeon who flew into the island for a week every six weeks, and that she was English.

Big help!

Although her being English *did* make it possible he'd met her before, as he'd been based in London all his working life.

It was now six weeks since the cocktail party to celebrate the opening of the luxury resort and the reopening of the research station funded by him in the same small piece of paradise.

Six weeks, and here he was back on Wildfire when he should be at another research facility he'd set up in

West Africa, or in Malaysia, organising the mosquito eradication programme. Should have been anywhere but here.

Brooding!

Enough!

He picked up his phone and got through to the island's small hospital.

'Is Dr Watson there?' he asked the woman who answered.

'Finished for the day, probably down on Sunset Beach,' was the succinct reply.

Sunset Beach—just around the corner, a short walk to the rock fall that separated his resort beach from the next small curve of sand. Walk around that and there was Sunset Beach.

He'd meet her there, as if by accident, and work out where they'd met—ask her again if necessary.

Action was better than brooding.

He dropped the phone and left the bure, not giving himself time to consider what he was doing in case he decided it wasn't a good idea.

He'd see her, ask her again where they'd met, perhaps smell her hair...

Was he mad?

Wasn't he in enough trouble with women at the moment, with his mother, three sisters, seven aunts, and Yasmina, the woman he was supposed to be marrying —for the good of the country, of course—insisting he come home and prepare to take over his role as ruler when his aging father died?

They all knew, as did his father, that his younger brother would be a far better ruler than he, and the very thought of returning home to the fussing of his horde of relatives made him feel distinctly claustrophobic.

While marriage to a stranger... That was something else.

He's spent too long in the West but deep in his bones knew that some of the old ways were best.

Some!

He was at the rock fall now.

Stupid! He should have stopped to put something on his feet as the rocks were sharp in places. But the tide was going out, the water at the base not very deep.

He'd wade...

Sarah came out of the cool, translucent water, towelled dry, then slipped her arms into the long white shirt she wore as covering over her swimsuit. Even at sunset the tropical sun had enough heat in it to burn her fair skin.

Fair skin and red hair—a great combination given she was slowly finding peace and contentment on this tropical island. Slowly putting herself back together again; finding a way forward in a life that had been shattered four years ago, sending her to what seemed like the end of the earth—Australia—and then finding a job where she could move around—a week here, a week there—not settling long enough for anyone to dig into her past, bring back the memories...

A loud roar of what had to be pain startled her out of her reverie and she looked towards the rock fall at the other end of the beach where a man—the roarer, apparently—was hopping up and down in thigh-deep water.

Some kind of local ritual?

No, it was definitely pain she'd heard—and could still hear.

Pushing her feet into her sandals, she ran across the white coral sand to where the man was struggling to get out of the water, clutching one foot now, slowly becoming the man she'd seen briefly at the cocktail party— the man they'd all called Harry.

Sheikh Rahman al-Taraq, in fact, a man she'd once admired enormously for the expertise and innovations he'd brought to paediatric surgery. Admired enough to be flattered when he'd asked her to have a coffee with him afterwards, babbling on to him about her desire to specialise in the same surgery. So she had been late for David, who'd said he'd wait at work and drive her home rather than letting her take the tube—half an hour late—half an hour, which could have changed everything.

She closed her eyes against the memories—the crash, the fear, the blood…

It hadn't been Harry's fault, of course, but how could she remember that meeting without all the horror of it coming back—not when she was healing, not on the island that had brought peace to her soul.

But right now that man was in pain.

She reached him and slipped to the side of what was his obviously injured foot, taking his arm and hauling it around her shoulders to steady him.

'What happened?' she asked, once they were stabilised in the now knee-deep water.

'Trod on something—agonising pain.'

The man's face was a pale, grimacing mask.

'Let's get you back to civilisation where we can phone the hospital,' she said, hoping she sounded more practical than she felt because the warmth of the man's body was disturbing her.

In fact, the man was disturbing her, and, if truth be told, the memory of her chance meeting with him at the cocktail party had been niggling inside her for the past six weeks. Reminding her of things she didn't want to remember…

But reminding her of other things, as well.

Not that he'd know that.

'I'm Sarah. We met at the cocktail party.'

'Harry!'

The name came out through gritted teeth but they were out of the water now and heading slowly, step hop, step hop, for the first of the bures in the resort.

'Did you see what it was?' Sarah asked, thinking of the many venomous inhabitants that lurked around coral reefs.

'Trod on it!'

They'd reached the door.

'That probably means a stonefish. They burrow down into the sand or camouflage themselves in rock pools so they're undetectable from their surroundings. You should be wearing shoes. Is your hot-water system good? Water hot?'

The man she was helping—Harry—seemed to swell with the rage that echoed in his voice.

'Need a shower, do you?'

Sarah decided that a man in pain was entitled to be a little tetchy so she ignored him, helping him to a chair and kneeling in front of him to examine his foot.

'You've got two puncture wounds and they're already swelling. I'll get some hot water and then phone the hospital. Hot water, as hot as you can stand, should ease the pain.'

Sarah looked directly at him, probably for the first

time since she'd arrived at the bottom of the rock fall. Even with gritted teeth and a fierce expression of pain on his face, he was good looking. Tall, dark, and handsome, like a prince in story books. The words formed in her head as she hurried to the small kitchen area of the bure in search of a bowl and hot water.

No bowls, but a large beaten copper vase. The stings were in the upper part of his foot—he could get that much of his foot into it.

Back at the chair, she knelt again, setting down the vase of hot water but keeping hold of the jug of cold water she'd brought with her.

'Try that with the toe of your good foot,' she said. 'If it's too hot I'll add cold water but you need it as hot as you can manage.'

He dipped a toe in and withdrew it quickly, tried again after Sarah had added water, and actually sighed with relief as he submerged the wounds in the container and the pain eased off.

Looking up at her, he shook his head.

'How did you know that?'

But she was on the phone to the hospital and someone had answered, so she could only shrug in reply to his question.

Quickly she explained the situation, turning back to Harry to ask, 'Is the pain travelling up your leg?'

He nodded.

'Like pins and needles that turn into cramp, although it's easier now.'

Sarah relayed the description to Sam, who was on the hospital end of the phone.

'We'll pick up a few things and be right down,' Sam said. 'Put his foot in hot water.'

Sarah smiled to herself as she hung up, glad some tiny crevice of her brain had come up with the same information, although it had been at least ten years since she'd practised general medicine and, having been in England, had never encountered a stonefish sting before.

Grabbing the jug, she returned to the kitchen for more hot water, knowing that as the water cooled, the pain would return.

'I *did* know you before the cocktail party,' her patient said as she returned, his dark eyes on her face, unsettling her with the intensity of his focus. 'I remember now. You were at the talk I gave at GOSH on the use of transoesophageal echocardiography for infants. We had a coffee together afterwards.'

His voice challenged her to deny it a second time!

Great Ormond Street Hospital—GOSH—of course she'd been there. How could she ever forget? She'd been so excited to be invited because back then she'd been considering paediatric surgery, and listening to the mesmeric speaker—this man—had crystallised her ambition.

But further memories of that fateful day brought such anguish she couldn't stop herself hitting out at the man who'd provoked them.

'The man *I* had coffee with was one of the foremost paediatric surgeons in the world, an innovator and inventor, always finding new ways to help the most vulnerable but important people in our society—children. I know you've been sick, but still there's so much you could offer.'

She shouldn't have let fly like that, and knew it, so guilt now mixed with the anguish churning inside her.

The recipient of the tirade just sat there, eyes hooded and spots of colour on his cheeks as warning signs of anger.

'The cart from the hospital is here, I'll go,' she said, her voice still taut—angry—hurt…

Ashamed?

Yes, very, but—

She thought she might have got away, but as she stalked out the door, jug of hot water still clenched in her hand, the man spoke.

'Well, the woman *I* met was ambitious to do the same work!'

Sarah closed her eyes, feeling stupid, useless tears sliding down her cheeks, almost blinding her as she made her way back to the beach to collect her things.

She'd deserved that comment, lashing out at him the way she had, but his insistence she remember that day had brought back far too many memories—just when she was beginning to think she'd healed.

How could he have said that?

Something so personal, and obviously very hurtful.

Because her words had struck a nerve?

More like a knife in his chest, directly into the similar doubts he had about himself.

Doubts he refused to face…

Which was no excuse for him to hit back at her!

What was happening to him that he could say such a thing?

'Done something stupid, have you?'

Sam Taylor, senior doctor at the hospital, charged into the bure.

It was impossible to brood with Sam around! He was a cheerful, capable man, who deftly delivered an analgesic to the wounded foot before suggesting Harry move to the hospital so the wound could be cleaned, while the antivenin and any further pain relief could be given intravenously.

He helped Harry out to the small electric cart that was the common transport on the island, and drove them up the hill from the resort to the neat little hospital.

Out of the hot water, the analgesic yet to work, the cramping, burning pain returned to both Harry's foot and his lower leg. But his mind had other things to handle.

Despair that he'd flung those words at Sarah Watson returned. Ultra childish, that's all it had been. *Her* words had stung, probably because there was an element of truth in them. In fact, they'd gone so deep he'd hit back automatically, and from the way her face had grown even paler, he'd hurt her badly.

She hadn't deserved that, for all she'd earlier denied knowing him. She certainly hadn't deserved it after getting him back to the bure and providing pain-relieving first aid. With agonising pain shooting up his leg, he'd not have made it alone.

'You brooding over something or is it just the pain?' Sam asked, as they pulled up at the small hospital.

'I *don't* brood!' Harry snapped, then regretted it.

More to brood over!

'I didn't think so,' Sam said cheerfully. 'Come on, we'll get you inside.'

Keanu Russell, the second permanent doctor at the hospital, had appeared and with Sam helped Harry through the small emergency room and into a well-equipped treatment alcove.

Harry checked out the paraphernalia by the bed.

'All this for a sting? Or are the spines lodged in my foot? Is it one of the deadly marine creatures that seem to flourish in these parts?'

Sam smiled and shook his head.

'You're here because we have good monitoring equipment in here. We can hook you up to oxygen, use a pulse oximeter, and a self-inflating blood-pressure cuff. And with a few wires on your chest, the screen will tell us all we need to know. And no, it's not deadly. Just painful.'

'Tell me about it!' Harry grumbled. 'I see myself as a tough guy but it was all I could do to not whimper while Sarah was helping me to my bure.'

'Going to keep him in?' Keanu asked Sam, as the two men efficiently attached him to the monitoring equipment.

'Nah, he's strong, and he just told us he's tough, so he'll survive. We'll drip the antivenin in, let him rest for a while, check everything's working as it should be, then send him home. He might only be a surgeon but I reckon he knows enough general medicine to yell for us if he has any further problems.'

Harry had to smile at the laid-back, teasing attitude of these men who worked on the island. They did enormous good, providing medical assistance and support to the whole M'Langi group of islands. It was a complicated programme of clinic visits, preventative medicine, rescue work and emergency callouts, yet they made everything seem easy.

Maybe if he stayed here long enough, he might pick up some of the relaxed island vibe.

Impossible right now, though. The woman he'd just hurt was walking into the room, still in the long white shirt she wore over a black bathing suit, a black and white striped beach towel slung over her shoulder, and an obviously anxious expression on her face.

Anxious about his well-being?

Well, she *was* a doctor!

'Is he okay?' she asked Sam.

'Ask him yourself,' Sam retorted, and the sea-green eyes set in that pale creamy skin turned towards him, narrowing slightly.

'Are you?' she demanded.

'Hey, be nice. He's a patient,' Sam reminded her.

'Yours, not mine. I just happened to be there when he strolled through reef waters without anything on his feet.'

She didn't actually add *the idiot*, but the words hung in a bubble in the air between them.

But even with her contempt there for all to see, she was beautiful. He knew it was probably her colouring that he found so fascinating: the vibrant hair, the pale skin, the flashing green eyes. Things he'd noticed way back when they'd first met.

But now he sensed something deeper in her that drew him inexorably to her.

Hidden pain?

He knew all about *that*.

Didn't it stab him every day when he felt the tremor in his hand as he shaved?

So grow a beard, a mocking voice within suggested, and Harry closed his eyes, against the voice and the woman.

'I just popped in to make sure he'd made it safely up here,' the woman said. 'So, see you two tomorrow.'

Sam stopped her retreat with a touch on her arm.

Harry suppressed a growl that rose in his throat. It had hardly been a lover's touch and, anyway, what business of his was it who touched her?

'Actually, Sarah,' Sam was saying, 'if you could spare a few minutes, I'd like you to stay around until the drip's finished. We were actually at a staff meeting up at the house and your phone call switched through to there. Mina's here for the other patients, but I think Harry should be watched.'

I have to *watch* him?

Sarah nodded in reply to Sam's request, telling herself it didn't mean *watch* watch, just to check on him now and then.

But watching him—he'd opened his eyes briefly as Sam spoke but they were closed again—actually *looking* at him might be a good idea. She could start by confirming her impressions of his physical appearance and maybe that would help sort out why the man made her so uneasy.

Why he stirred responses deep inside her that she hadn't felt for four years…

For sure he was good looking. Olive-skinned, dark-haired, strong face, with a straight nose and solid chin. The lips softened it just a little, beautifully shaped—sensual—

Get with it, Sarah!

Stop this nonsense!

'Are you looking at me?'

Surprisingly pale eyes—grey—opened, and black eyebrows rose.

'Not looking, just watching—that's what I was asked to do, remember.'

'Not much difference, I'd have thought,' the wretch said, with the merest hint of a smile sliding across those sens—

His lips!

She turned her attention to the monitor. The blood-pressure cuff was just inflating, so at least she had something to watch.

A little high, but the pain would only just be subsiding, so that was to be expected.

'Tell me if you feel any reaction to the antivenin,' she told him. 'Nausea, faintness...'

He opened one eye and raised the eyebrow above it as if to say, is that all you've got?

She almost smiled then realised smiling at this man might be downright dangerous, so she walked out into the main room and found a magazine that was only four years old, grabbed a chair, and returned with it to the emergency cubicle to sit as far as possible from the man as she could get in the curtained alcove and still see the monitor.

He appeared to be asleep, and she tried hard to give her full attention to an article about the various cosmetic procedures currently in vogue in the US.

And failed.

The stonefish wound was in his right foot, so it had been his right arm she'd had around her shoulder as she'd taken some of his weight to get him back to the bure.

Had she felt a tremor in it?

Looking at him now, the arm in question was lying still on the bed. Or was it gripping the bed?

Parkinson's patients she'd encountered in the past found tremors in their arms and hands worsened when they relaxed but lessened when they held something. Would that hold true for tremors induced by encephalitis or was a different part of the brain affected?

And just why was she interested?

She sighed and tried to tell herself it was because the surgery world had been shocked to learn the results of his brush with encephalitis. Shocked that such a talented and skilful man had been lost to surgery.

But she wasn't here to wonder about his tremor. That was his business.

She was here to watch him, not worry about his past or the problems he faced now.

She turned her attention from the monitor to the man.

His eyes were open, studying her in turn, and although she'd have liked to turn away, she knew doing so would be an admission that he disturbed her.

'I'm sorry,' he said, those strange pale eyes holding hers. 'I had no right to throw such a petty, personal, ridiculous remark at you. All my friends tell me I'm over-sensitive about the results of my illness, but that's no excuse.'

Now she did look instead of watching, looked and saw the apology mirrored in his eyes.

She almost weakened because the man had been through hell.

And to a certain extent hadn't she opted out as well, heading away from home as fast as she could, taking a job that meant she didn't have to settle in one place, make friends, get hurt by loss again?

But she hadn't been a genius at what she did and this man had. The world needed him and people like him.

Straightening her shoulders, she met his eyes and said, 'Well, if you're expecting an apology from me, forget it. I meant every word I said. You must have any number of minions who could run around checking on the facilities and programmes you've sent up. By doing it yourself, you're wasting such skill and talent it's almost criminal.'

And on that note she would have departed, except she was stuck there—watching him.

Watching him raise that mobile eyebrow once again. 'Minions?'

The humour lurking in the word raised her anger.

'You know exactly what I mean,' she snapped, and he nodded.

Thinking she'd got the last word, she prepared to depart, or at least back as far away as possible from him.

'But we *had* met before—you'll admit that now!' he said.

So much for having the last word! He'd not only sneaked that one in but he'd brought back the memories—of that wonderful day at GOSH *and* the horror of its aftermath.

Her heart was beating so fast it was a wonder the patient couldn't hear it, and a sob of anguish wasn't far away. The curtain sliding back saved her from total humiliation as she burst into tears in front of this man.

Caroline Lockhart, one of the permanent nurses at the hospital, appeared, flashing such a happy smile that Sarah couldn't not smile back at her.

'I'm to take over,' Caroline said quietly. 'Sam says thanks for the hand. We were discussing how best to spend a rather large donation we've just received—working out what's needed most. Since you overwhelmed us with the equipment needed for endoscopies and keyhole surgery, the theatre's pretty well sorted. But if you have any other ideas, let someone know.'

Sarah nodded and stood up, wanting to get as far away as possible. Caroline's words had added a further layer to her pain. Getting compensation for the accident that had taken her husband and unborn child four years after the event had been traumatic to say the least—how could money possibly replace a husband and son?—so her immediate reaction had been to get rid of it as quickly as possible.

And because it was the leisurely pace and overwhelming beauty of this magic island where she'd finally begun to put the broken pieces of herself back together again, wasn't it right she give something back?

She made her way out of the rear of the hospital, down to the little villa where she stayed when she was here, and tapped on the door of the villa next door to remind her anaesthetist they had an early start in the morning.

Ben was clad in board shorts, his hair ruffled and a vague expression on his face.

'Did I catch you at a bad moment?' she asked.

'Halfway through dismembering a body,' he replied, and Sarah grinned.

Ben was an excellent anaesthetist and didn't mind the travel, but apparently he was an even better writer, his sixth murder mystery hitting top-seller lists. It was only a matter of time before he was making enough money from his writing to support himself and she'd have to find a new anaesthetist willing to travel to isolated places in outback Queensland, and to Wildfire in the M'Langi group of islands.

'We're doing that thyroidectomy tomorrow. You all set?' she asked.

He raised his hand in a mocking salute.

'Ready as ever, ma'am,' he said, the words telling her he was still lost in his book—one of his characters talking.

But lost though he was at the moment, she knew he'd be fully focussed in the morning.

'Our patient came in this afternoon, if you want to pop over the hospital tonight to talk to her. I'd say the op will take three to four hours, depending on any complications, and she's had some complications with her heart so we'll have to watch her.

Ben nodded.

'Don't worry, we'll be right. I've already read up on her and checked with my old boss back in Sydney about the level of drug use. We'll be fine.'

Ben was about to back away, obviously anxious to get back to what he considered his real work, when he paused, then reached out and touched her cheek.

'Have you been crying?' There was suspicion and a touch of anger in his voice, and in his eyes. 'Did someone upset you?'

Sarah forced a smile onto her lips and fixed it there. She was only too aware of how protective Ben was of her, once taking on the boss of an outback hospital when he'd wanted her to work beyond regulation safe hours.

'I'm fine,' she told him, taking his hand from her cheek and giving his fingers a 'thank you' squeeze.

'Well, I hope you are,' he said, before disappearing back into his villa, from which Sarah could almost hear his computer calling to him.

But the little white lie had made her feel better, so

instead of hiding away in her island home, she walked to the top of the cliffs above Sunset Beach to catch the last fiery blast of the sunset.

Except she'd missed it. The soft pinks and mauves and violets, however, were still stunningly beautiful and like a soothing balm to her aching heart.

CHAPTER TWO

KEANU DROVE HARRY back to his bure, offering to stay for a while, though Harry could see he was itching to get into the newly refurbished laboratories. As well as Harry's team working towards clinical trials of an encephalitis vaccine, other scientists were welcome to use the facilities, and Keanu's passion at the moment—apart from his fiancée, Caroline, and saving the island's gold mine—was examining the properties of M'Langi tea, a project started by his father many years ago.

'Are you getting anywhere?' Harry asked the young doctor.

Keanu shook his head.

'We know we have fewer encephalitis cases than other South Sea islands and the only difference as far as diet is concerned is this tea we drink.'

Harry nodded.

Keanu's work fitted with what his team was doing, but the two strands needed to be studied separately.

Keanu pulled up outside the bure and came around to help Harry inside.

But he sat for a moment, wondering if he might not be better off going up to the lab, making himself useful.

Or would he be a nuisance to his 'minions', as Sarah Watson had described them?

Of course he would, limping and still in some pain as he was. Besides, meticulous research work was not his thing—he was far too impatient.

Though not in surgery…

'Thanks, Keanu, I can hop from here,' he said, waving away the man's assistance, his traitorous mind thinking of the last person who'd helped him inside the building.

Maybe it was lemons, not vinegar—or something a little tarter…

Limes?

Hobbling up the two steps, his foot still in pain, he shook his head at his stupidity. Sarah had made her feelings clear when she'd let fly about his behaviour, neither could he have failed to feel the contempt in her words.

Deserved contempt?

Probably!

Forget the woman!

Easier said than done.

Women usually lingered pleasantly in his head, small, special moments of past relationships stored neatly away like boxes in a storeroom in his brain.

But this woman…

No way she'd stay in a box!

Perhaps because they *hadn't* had a relationship.

They'd been nothing more than ships that had passed in the night!

She'd been pregnant. She obviously had a family— husband and child—or at least the child.

So why the job of flying surgeon?

She'd be home, what, one week in four or five? Hardly a good arrangement for family life.

And none of his business...

Sarah loved operating in the small but brilliant theatre at Wildfire. Double-glazed windows let in natural light while allowing the room to be airconditioned, and through them she could see the tangle of treetops and vines in the rainforest that ran up the hill behind the hospital.

Added to which Sam was an excellent assistant, competent in his own right to perform routine operations but unable to take time out of his busy schedule to do regular surgical work. Hettie, the head nurse, and Caroline both enjoyed theatre nursing so, with Ben, she had a great team.

The patient was sedated, breathing through an endotracheal tube, and Sarah was about to begin when she sensed, rather than saw, another person enter the room.

Sensed who it was, too.

'Glad you felt well enough to come up,' Sam said cheerfully to the newcomer, who was still somewhere behind Sarah as she lifted a scalpel off the tray, ready to begin. 'It's not often we can show off our theatre to someone who's seen the best.'

'Thank you for inviting me.'

The deep voice reverberated down Sarah's spine, and she had to focus on the lines she'd drawn on the patient's neck and breathe deeply for a moment to steady her nerves.

Sam glanced at her, the retractors in his hand, ready to begin, while Hettie shifted a little impatiently, ready to cauterise tiny blood vessels.

Sarah began, although a tiny portion of her mind was protesting that it was *her* theatre right now and she could ask him to leave.

When the hospital boss had invited him?

She focussed fully on the patient, cutting into the throat in a crease in the woman's neck so the scar would be next to invisible. The parathyroid glands lay directly behind the thyroid, so at the forefront of her mind her brain was locating and isolating them so they wouldn't be damaged.

The area was also filled with important nerves and blood vessels, not to mention the larynx, just above the gland, so it was easy to lose herself in the meticulous work, excluding all outside factors.

Three hours later the glands had been removed and Sarah was checking they'd cauterised all the blood vessels in the incision.

'I'll close for you if you like,' Sam offered, and, knowing how much he enjoyed being part of the surgery, Sarah stepped back, only too happy to let him finish the job.

'Do you want a drain in place?" he asked, and she checked the open wound again.

'No, it's clean,' she said. 'Good job, team.'

She crossed the theatre towards the washrooms, stripping off her gloves and gown and dumping them in a bin by the door. Still clad in the highly unflattering green hospital scrubs, she turned to push her way through the door, finally catching sight of the unexpected onlooker.

He'd obviously been masked as he'd stood outside the sterile area of the theatre. Now the white strip of paper hung around his neck, resting on the collar of a dark blue polo shirt that clung to a chest any athlete would be proud to display.

And just why had she been looking at his chest?

To avoid looking at his face?

Probably!

But what was it about the man that drew her eyes?

More than her eyes… Her senses.

Forget him!

She felt strongly about his opting out of the world of paediatric surgery. From all she'd seen and read, he'd been truly gifted.

And he'd made her cry!

Twice!

So why was she even thinking about him?

She stripped off her clothes, showered, and pulled on a pair of white slacks and a black and white striped tee that was old and faded but very soft and comforting. Pushing her feet into sandals, she went out the back door of the changing room and along the corridor to the rear of the hospital, heading for her villa.

Ben was in charge of their patient now, and would keep an eye on her in the recovery room. Sarah would see her in the morning.

The first thing she saw as she walked into the villa was the jug from Harry's bure—the jug she'd carried away with her as she'd fled the man's taunt.

Well, he was up at the hospital with Sam right now, so she'd duck down to the resort and leave it outside his door. She grabbed her hat, a large droopy-brimmed black creation, off the hook by the door.

The ducking down to his island home would have

worked if he hadn't overtaken her as she strolled down
the track, admiring the beautiful, lush gardens and isolated bures.

Finding he'd lost interest in the hospital once Sarah had
departed, Harry made his way across the airstrip and
onto the track that led through the resort.

The figure striding ahead of him was instantly recognisable despite the floppy black hat covering her glorious hair.

Glorious hair?

He really was losing it with this woman…

This woman he'd hurt when he'd hit out at her.

Unforgiveable, really.

'Going my way?'

She started at his voice, but perhaps because it was
such a corny thing to say she also smiled and held up
the jug.

'Returning your property, but now you're here I can
give it to you.'

She turned towards him, pushing the jug into his
hands, their fingers touching, time suspended.

'Have lunch with me?'

The invitation coming out like it had startled *him*,
and apparently was so unexpected Sarah could only
peer up at him from under the hat.

What did she see?

His regret?

Or had she heard a hint of desperation in his voice?
She thought for a moment then said yes.

She seemed as startled as he'd been by the acceptance, but he couldn't hide his pleasure, smiling as he
took her elbow to walk her down the track.

His foot still pained him but he tried to hide it, then wondered if was kindness because he *was* limping that had made her say yes and hadn't shaken off his hand.

Probably!

Harry's light touch on her elbow was causing Sarah's body all the same manifestations of attraction she'd first felt as she'd helped him out of the water the previous day.

The same manifestations that had *so* confused her she'd ranted at the man about his life choice!

He didn't speak until they'd reached his island home. He walked her through the room where she'd given him first aid and out to a trellis-covered deck.

He waved his hand towards a cushioned cane chair, then sat down opposite her, looking at her, studying her as she pulled off the hat and shook out her hair—studying her as if to really look at her was the sole reason he'd brought her there.

The strange part was she didn't mind, not when it gave her time to study him—to try to work out just what was at play here.

A subliminal link from the past—back when *both* their lives had been so different?

Or something more basic, even earthy… Simple attraction?

Was attraction ever simple?

And not having experienced it for so long, how could she be sure that's what it was?

'Cold drink? Juice?' he finally asked, and Sarah wondered if she'd imagined that brief moment of mutual interest.

'Cold water would be great,' she said, then sank thankfully back into the chair as he disappeared inside.

Relief washed through her but it didn't entirely release the inner tension she was feeling—or the strange, almost magnetic force this man exerted over her.

Saying yes to lunch—sitting staring at him—this wasn't her. Sarah Watson was practical, organised, totally self-contained, and content with the new life she'd made for herself.

He reappeared carrying a large tray, the jug she'd just returned set in the middle of it, surrounded by platters of sliced tropical fruit, curls of finely cut meat, chunks of cheese and a cane basket filled with soft rolls and bruschetta.

'One moment,' he said, disappearing inside again, then reappearing with plates, glasses, cutlery, napkins and a smaller tray containing little dishes of butter and relishes.

'Wow? You did all this in a matter of minutes?' Sarah said, looking up at him as he checked they had everything they needed.

'Minions,' he said briefly, placing a plate and glass in front of her. 'The resort staff bring me a lunch this size every day, although I keep telling them there's only one of me and I can't possibly eat it all.'

'So you asked me to lunch to help you out?' Sarah teased, looking up at him.

He held her gaze for an instant then shook his head.

'Heaven only knows why I asked you to lunch,' he growled, a puzzled frown drawing his dark eyebrows together. 'It just seemed to come out of me, but as both Sam and Caroline have ripped strips off me for upsetting you, maybe my conscience made the call.'

So Sam *had* seen her crying as she'd left the bure, and Caroline had definitely seen she'd been upset in the ER yesterday…

But tearing strips off him?

She concentrated on the lunch, forking some sliced fruit onto her plate, taking a piece of bruschetta, some cheese—

'You obviously know my recent history, but what happened to you?' he asked, his voice gentler now, his eyes on hers, not on the plate already filled with meat and cheese that he was holding in his hand.

She frowned at the intrusive question, selected a piece of melon, didn't answer.

'You don't have to answer, of course, but I've obviously upset you, and I wouldn't knowingly do that. Not for the world.'

She *had* to look at him now, and she saw not only concern but empathy in his eyes.

It would be so easy to tell him, to excuse her rudeness to him by revealing why remembering the night they'd first met had caused her so much pain.

Yet still she hesitated, until he moved his chair closer, lifted the plate from her hands and set it on the table, then took one of her hands in both of his and looked deep into her eyes.

'What happened to your ambition to practise paediatric surgery, to the child you carried? What was so terrible it sent you halfway across the world to take on the itinerant work you do?'

His words were almost hesitant, so much so she knew it wasn't curiosity but some deeper need to know.

The same need to know that she felt about him—a need to know more of this man.

Although she left her hand where it was, she couldn't look at him, chewing at the melon when it had already dissolved to mush in her mouth.

'I watched you today,' he continued, genuine interest in his voice. 'You're a natural surgeon, the instruments are like extensions of your fingers, and your hands move almost without messages from your brain. You were so enthusiastic about paediatric surgery—'

'So were you!' She shot the reminder at him. 'Stuff happens, as well you know.'

He didn't reply, studying her again, then gave a rough shake of his head.

'I'm sorry, I really hadn't meant to bring all this up, to pry into your private life. It's none of my business what you do or why you do it and if I hurt you yesterday I'm truly sorry.'

Sarah met his eyes, and saw the apology there as well, but behind it the questions lingered, questions she didn't want to answer—probably couldn't.

Not right now, anyway...

Harry moved his chair away—fractionally—then picked up the plate he'd removed from Sarah's hands and gave it back to her.

Was he out of his mind? Here he had the company of this attractive woman and he'd ruined the lunch by demanding to know why her life had changed.

He'd already upset her twice, obviously by the things he'd said about the past, so why was he pushing for answers she equally obviously didn't want to give?

And why should she?

What business was it of his what she did or why she did it?

He was attracted to her—he'd got that far in sorting things out—but he'd rarely, or possibly never, pried into the pasts of other women to whom he'd been attracted.

He had accepted them as they were, enjoying a relationship that brought pleasure to both of them, always with the understanding that that was all it would ever be.

He knew some of the reasons it was all the women concerned wanted—their careers came first, or they'd been hurt before and just wanted the fun and companionship, and, yes, sex.

While ever conscious that for all he'd built his own life away from his family and the place of his birth, he still had obligations there—and a woman his family had pledged him to marry.

So relationships had been, well, fun, and many of the women remained his friend.

But this woman?

He pushed his plate away, his appetite gone, and looked at her.

'For all we seem to have done nothing but fling accusations at each other and probably hurt each other more than we should, there's something between us,' he said, hoping that bringing things out into the open might help.

She smiled, which didn't help.

'You mean a cup of coffee nearly five years ago and a stonefish sting?'

'No!'

He hadn't meant to snap, but even in his own ears it sounded snappy.

'A link, an attraction—a strong attraction that I think you can feel, too.'

She looked up from her plate then looked down again, very deliberately choosing a slice of pineapple and lifting it to luscious pink lips.

Every sinew in his body tightened—attraction? Or nerves about what, if anything, she might reply?

'And?' she said finally, when she'd chewed the pineapple far more than was necessary and swallowed it, the white skin on her throat moving up and down, the tip of her tongue sliding out to wipe the juice from her lips.

The tightening this time definitely wasn't nerves.

'And what?' The words scratched out from a throat thickened by emotion.

She almost smiled, her lips widening just slightly, indenting the faintest of dimples into her cheeks.

'And what would we do about it if, as you say, there's something there?'

'I don't know!'

He threw up his arms in exasperation. This wasn't how his courtships usually worked. He met a woman, they liked each other, went out for dinner then usually ended up in bed.

No, he shouldn't have thought about the bed part, especially as his bed was so close and he could already picture a naked Sarah Watson spread out on it, while he licked the cream of her skin from her toes to her forehead.

Possibly pausing on the way, here and there...

He blanked the image and forced his mind to shut down the thoughts accompanying it.

'It's a long time since I've been in a relationship,' she said quietly, setting down her plate and leaning back in the chair, the faded T-shirt she was wearing pulling tight against her full breasts.

'Because?'

He *had* to ask but all she did was shake her head and look so lost he wanted to scoop her into his arms and hold her tight against his chest until the sadness left her lovely eyes.

'But I probably wouldn't mind one.'

Had he heard her right?

'With me?' he managed to get out, any semblance of the suave man of the world he thought himself completely gone.

This time she smiled properly.

'Well, you're here, and I think you're right, there *is* something between us, isn't there? We're both old enough to recognise attraction, and should be able to admit to it, for all it's weird when neither of us seem to *like* each other particularly, and I don't really believe in instant...'

'Lust?' he suggested when she faltered in her almost clinical dissection of what lay between them.

'I suppose that's as good a word for what we're experiencing as any,' she admitted, 'and given I'm only here for a week—well, five days now—it wouldn't have time to get complicated. It'd be like a holiday romance only without the holiday part—a fling.'

He nodded, partly because he couldn't find the words but also, in part, because he had no idea where to go from there.

Taking her into the bedroom and peeling off all her clothes was one option, but it seemed a little abrupt—even more clinical than her words had been.

Damn it all, how did he usually get a woman into

bed? He must have some technique—some idea of how to get from a shared lunch to the bedroom!

She was smiling, probably at the confusion that must be evident on his face.

Had she *really* just suggested they have an affair—well, hardly an affair, surely they took longer…?

I wouldn't mind one. She'd definitely said that.

Put the words right out there in the open, in a cartoon bubble above her head!

Well, the man *was* the most handsome, sexy member of the species she'd ever met, and if you counted tingling nerves, and a racing pulse, and shallow breathing, then he was right about there being something between them.

But an affair?

Well, hardly that, a fling.

A very short fling…

What the hell!

She looked into those slumberous grey eyes, studied the moulded lips, and, as panic yelled at her to go, to run for her life, she heard herself saying, 'Well, what happens next?'

He looked so stunned, she helped him out.

'Either I kiss you or you kiss me, I guess. Do you have a preference?'

He made a growling kind of noise and drew her close, studying her face, running his fingers through her hair, eyes wide now with a kind of wonder.

'You're serious?'

'Well, I think I am, but the more you mess about the more worried I'm getting. Perhaps we should sleep on it, decide tomorrow.'

This time the growly noise was more like a purr.

'And miss tonight? No way.'

Now, finally, he *did* kiss her.

Well, she guessed it was just a kiss, although it was unlike anything she'd ever experienced, sending her brain cells into a muzzy cloud and her body into a frenzy of desire.

Lust?

What the hell? Did it really matter?

She concentrated on the kiss, on kissing him with as much heat as he was kissing her.

Kissing *him*...

He felt her momentary hesitation, remembered her tears, and lifted his head, cupping her face in his hands, and looked into her eyes.

'You're sure about this?'

Well, nearly sure...

She didn't say the words but he read it in her eyes. Nearly sure wasn't good enough—not this time, for some reason, not with this woman.

Though at other times would he have hesitated?

Hell, what did *he* know?

Except he wanted her to be sure, so he kissed her lightly on the lips and tried a smile, although he knew it probably looked as false as it felt.

'Think about it,' he said quietly.

She eased her body away from his and nodded.

'I think I need to,' she responded.

And with that, she stood up, thanked him politely for the lunch, and walked away.

Out of his bure, but not out of his life?

He had no idea...

CHAPTER THREE

SARAH HEADED STRAIGHT for the rock fall. Sunset Beach was her sanctuary on this island and the sooner she got there the sooner she might be able to work out why she'd suddenly taken leave of her senses.

Calmly telling that man she wouldn't mind an affair! That *was* what she'd said, wasn't it?

And from what part of her obviously impaired brain had those words sprung?

Although, remembering the heat of that one long kiss, she doubted her brain had had anything to do with it.

Even so...

She was clambering over the rocks now as the tide was in, but her mind raced to find an explanation for her behaviour.

Once on the beach she sat in the shade of the rocks— it was really far too early for her to be out here—and let the beauty of that special place calm her racing heart.

In the beginning, all she'd had room for in her heart and mind had been her grief, the grieving process isolating her from others, so she'd barely noticed that the sensual part of her nature had died along with David and her unborn child.

But seeing Rahman al-Taraq—Harry—again at the cocktail party had not only brought back memories of that dreadful day but, contrarily, had reawoken her senses. She'd been so startled by the unmistakable surge of attraction she'd felt towards him that she'd denied ever having met him and fled the party.

Yet, once reawoken and stirred, those parts of her that had lain dormant would no longer be denied, and over the following weeks she'd dreamt, at times, not particularly of Harry but of the pleasant, teasing sex she'd shared with David, although sometimes in the dreams he wasn't David, and sometimes in the dreams she'd wanted more…

She shook her head, sighed, and stared out at the translucent water that ran over the reef through the lagoon and splashed on the beach near her feet.

Was it because she'd finally got her life back in order—had put herself together again, albeit like a jigsaw with more than a few pieces missing—that her libido had returned?

Whatever!

It wasn't the whys and wherefores of her returning hormonal rush that she had to consider but what she was going to do about it.

Have a brief affair?

A fling?

Get it out of her system?

But could that happen?

Might she not want more?

She sighed again then reminded herself that if she did there were other men out there—for companionship, a bit of fun and pleasant, perhaps even exciting, sex.

She glanced up at the sky, hoping that wherever David's spirit was he wasn't privy to her thoughts.

Then she smiled!

It was David who'd taught her it was okay to enjoy sex—more than okay. David who'd taught her it could be fun as well as unbelievably intense.

David...

Harry felt as if he'd been pacing his room for hours. The woman—Sarah—had calmly told him she wouldn't mind having an affair then, equally calmly, had walked away.

Well, probably not as calmly—that kiss had been *hot*!

What made it worse was that she hadn't actually said it was him she wouldn't mind having an affair with!

No, she'd just wandered off as if the whole almost clinical discussion had never happened.

He had to find out.

Would she be at the beach?

He'd been told she went there at sunset every day when she was on the island, but today?

His body was so taut with wanting her he felt the slightest bump might shatter it. He'd been okay until she'd more or less said yes.

He tried to analyse his feelings.

Attracted, yes.

Desire spiralling within him, definitely.

But strung tight like this?

This was new and he was unsure what it meant.

Best not to think about it. Go around to the beach—with something on his feet—and see if she was there.

He saw her as he reached the rock fall, long white

arms stroking rhythmically through the water, little splashes as her feet kicked, her wet hair appearing almost black against her pale skin.

He crossed the small sandy area to where her clothes were piled under a pandanus palm and picked up her towel, carrying it down to the water's edge and waiting for her to come out.

She rose like Venus from her shell, shaking her head to clear the water from her hair, the paleness of her skin seeming lighter against the black swimsuit that moulded a perfect body with full breasts, a narrow waist drawing the eye to her hips and from there to her long, long legs...

She looked up, saw him—and smiled.

The tightness in his body zeroed downwards, and his hands trembled as he draped the towel around her shoulders, holding it closed beneath her chin.

'You're shaking,' she murmured, looking up into his face, perhaps reading the naked need he was feeling.

'You've bewitched me,' he muttered, his reaction to this woman so strong he wondered if maybe the encephalitis had returned and he was delirious.

He breathed deeply, calming himself, then wrapped the towel completely around her, leaving his hands at the back of her waist, easing her body closer.

Kissing was close, but for now it was enough to hold her, more than enough that she didn't push away...

Sea-green eyes looked up into his and her pink lips widened into a shy smile.

'This is weird.'

The words were little more than a breath of air, but her face told him so much more. She was uncertain, vulnerable...

And he wanted to hold her forever.

'You wanted something?'

She'd shifted slightly and her lost look had been re-placed by a mischievous grin.

'You!' he muttered gruffly, although he knew he was rushing things.

This woman wasn't one of the career-focussed busi-nesswomen with whom he usually dallied, and he, for certain, wasn't, right now, the attentive, caring, casual lover *he* usually was.

That man had romance and seduction down pat, while the man on the beach right now, the man in his skin, was so damned uncertain he was *shaking*.

She'd eased away from him, dried herself—hell, he should have done that, not stood there holding her. *He* should have been running that towel down her legs, over her curves, drying the pale skin between her shoulder blades.

For the first time in his life he understood the phrase 'pull yourself together'. It had always seemed asinine to him, but right now it was what he needed to do.

As she dropped the towel on the beach he recovered sufficiently to reach down for the shirt he knew she wore over her swimsuit, then hold it for her, watching her slide long, slim arms into the sleeves, turning her gently so he could button the shirt, right there above the swell of her breasts.

He could barely breathe as his fingers brushed against her skin, and felt her tension as she stood, statue-still beneath his touch.

'Have dinner with me.'

He'd meant it to be a request but it had come out as a demand.

Expecting her to be offended, he was surprised when she relaxed and moved just a little away from him, smiling as she said, 'Minions do dinner, too?'

He hoped the wild swoop of pleasure he felt wasn't making him look like an idiot as he smiled in turn.

'It's that kind of resort. I can order anything. What do you fancy? The crayfish is particularly good at the moment.'

'I'll try it,' she said, then she bent down to spread the towel on the sand, slapped the huge hat she wore onto her head, and straightened to look at him again.

'What time?'

There was a challenge in the words and he guessed it was aimed more at herself than at him. It had been a while, she'd said, and now she was obviously nervous.

But game!

He liked that, liked it a lot.

But then, there were so many things he was beginning to like about this woman...

'Will you stay and watch the sunset with me?'

As soon as Sarah had said the words she regretted them. As an invitation they weren't in the same league as 'Have dinner with me', but on top of that, didn't she usually enjoy the splendour of the sunset on her own?

Wasn't it *her* special moment of the day?

'I'd like that.'

Her gut twisted. Things were really getting out of hand when she was having physical reactions to three simple words.

And now she'd asked him, would she have to share the towel?

He solved that problem by dropping to the ground

beside her towel and picking up a handful of the coarse coral sand.

'So white,' he murmured, as she settled beside him. 'Not as fine as the sand back home, but beautiful in its own way.'

He'd turned to look at her as he'd said the last phrase but she refused to take the words personally.

'For real beauty we have to wait,' she said, nodding to where the sun seemed to be almost diving towards the horizon, the sky around it a brilliant red and gold. 'As it drops lower the colours in the sky reflect not only on the water but on crystals in the sand, as well. I've seen it pink and red and even purple at times. A painted world!'

He nodded, and she wondered about his country, about his apparent exile from it, and whether the sunset painted the desert sand with colour...

And for the first time since the accident she felt curious about a place—felt an urge to travel, see a desert at sunset, maybe other wonders the world had to offer.

'Oh, yes,' he murmured, and she set her wayward thoughts aside.

Thin bands of cloud made the explosion of colour even more dramatic, the western sky alive with fire.

He took her hand and somehow that was okay.

Comfortable even, for they were sharing something special.

The colours faded to beautiful, hazy pinks and mauves, and Sarah stood reluctantly.

'Night falls swiftly,' she reminded him. 'I need to go so I can navigate the path safely.'

For some reason she was still holding his hand.

He had taken it to help her to her feet, so had her

hand just decided to stay there in his—warm and comfortable?

Seeking a distraction, she looked towards the now dark shadow of the rock fall.

'You shouldn't go back that way,' she told him. 'Come up the path and walk back down to the resort.'

He didn't answer, but walked with her to the foot of the path.

'I'd have walked you up anyway,' he said. 'I do have *some* manners.'

She paused on the first step on the path and looked down at him.

'You realise the jungle drums will be beating before long?'

He laughed, a rich, unexpectedly joyful sound that made her smile.

'So let them beat.' He came abreast of her and turned towards her, his voice softer as he added, 'Is that all right with you? Or will it make you uncomfortable?'

She smiled at his concern.

'I think I've been uncomfortable for years,' she told him, and took a deep breath to steel herself before continuing. 'They died, my husband and unborn son, in an accident, that same night I met you at GOSH. We were on our way home. Seeing you again—at the cocktail party—it brought it all back.'

'Oh, Sarah, what can I say?' He stepped up onto the narrow step, and put his arms around her. 'Nothing that would help, I do know that. I cannot even imagine such a loss, or the pain it must have caused you.'

She allowed herself to be held, perhaps even snuggled closer, the physical contact, the security of being held healing another bit of her that had been lost.

He kissed the top of her head, then asked gruffly, 'And since then?'

'People tiptoed around me, thought carefully about what they'd say, or didn't say much at all, which suited me just fine because I had no time for anything but grief.'

She eased away and climbed again, but this time with him in the lead and her hand still in his.

It had been too dark to see his face as she'd blurted out the past, but his voice had been so deep and understanding she caught up with him and stopped beside him.

Looked at him as she tried to find the words she needed.

'I've been busy putting myself back together—like a jigsaw, or a broken vase. Coming to Australia—as far as I could get from where my life had been—gave me the base, then slowly, bit by bit, I've got it just about done.'

'But pieces are still missing?' he asked, resting his hand on her cheek, his thumb wiping at a tear she hadn't realised was there.

'Oh, yes, pieces are missing.'

She smiled although she knew it was probably a weak effort, so she, in turn, laid her palm on *his* cheek.

'Even if nothing happens between us, you have given me another piece—the bit of me that can be stirred by a man—the bit that feels desire and lust. And it being a fling, well, that's right, too...'

She hesitated, unsure how to go on, surprised when he finished the words for her.

'Because losing love was too hurtful? Because you don't want to be hurt like that again?'

She pressed against him, silently acknowledging that

truth, feeling his arms around her, holding her safe from hurt for what seemed like a long time.

He kissed her then, just gently on the lips, demanding nothing but somehow making a promise of the kiss.

They turned and walked again.

'We're there now,' she said, and hoped he didn't hear the hoarseness of desire in her voice.

The man seemed to have unleashed a monster...

'My villa's second from the bottom. What time tonight?'

She was talking too fast, rattling out the words because she'd suddenly realised she had no idea how she *would* react to those jungle drums. Her private life had been private for so long, and now, inevitably, there would be talk.

Could she handle it?

'Eight o'clock?' she suggested, when he didn't answer. That would give her time to be alone, to think things through.

So many things...

'No, no, come earlier. We'll have a drink, talk. Come as soon as you're ready.'

He spoke quickly and Sarah realised he was as uncertain as she was about whatever it was that was happening between them, and somehow that made her like him more.

Not that she knew him, or anything much about him, apart from his illness and opting out of surgery.

'I'll just shower and change and walk down.'

He opened his mouth and she knew he was going to offer to come for her, to drive her down, but she put her finger to his lips and said, 'I'll walk. Jungle drums, remember?'

'And you think no one will notice you walking down to the resort?'

'They will, but I walk a lot, all over the place. "There goes Sarah again" is all they're likely to say.'

'And dinner? They won't miss you at dinner?'

Was he holding her here with fairly meaningless conversation because he didn't want them to part?

'I usually eat in my villa—I like simple meals and I'm in the habit of preparing them myself. Anything I can eat with a fork and keep reading whatever I happen to be reading while I eat.'

She knew it was time to turn away again, get inside to think, but she was enjoying standing there, looking at him, taking in the little details of this man she didn't know.

A faint white scar, like a crescent moon, on his cheek by his right ear, the little lines that played around the corners of his mouth as he smiled, the dark lashes that could hood his eyes in a split second, hiding any hint of emotion.

'Come soon,' he said quietly, and every nerve in her body ran with fire.

Harry wasn't sure how he felt as he headed back down past the laboratories and kitchens to go through the resort to his bure.

Hearing the bare bones of Sarah's story had probably cut into him more than if he'd had the details.

Not that he needed more information when he'd heard the pain still echoing in her words as she'd laid them matter-of-factly before him.

It made him want her more, yet warned him to be careful—to take this pursuit more slowly than he usually did, for, like a skittish horse, Sarah could, at any time, back away from him.

Which only made him want, even more, to hold her in his arms.

Hold her in his arms?

When had he ever wanted to do that with a woman? Apart from during foreplay or sex...

So he had to pull back, cool off, treat this as just another attraction, a fling for their mutual enjoyment.

Not get too involved...

He *never* got too involved, mainly because he knew he couldn't offer more than an affair. Eventually he'd have to give up his nomadic lifestyle—was he a modern-day throwback to his ancestors who'd roamed the desert on camels?—and return home, to duties and to a woman his family had chosen for him to marry...

'You and Sarah made up your differences?'

Sam had emerged from the shadows of the gardens around the laboratories, and Harry could only shake his head that the message of the jungle drums had spread so quickly.

Not that he intended to respond to Sam. Whatever it was that lay between himself and any woman was private. With Sarah, it felt even more intensely private.

'How's the research going?' he asked Sam instead, and his friend laughed.

'Well fielded,' he said, patting Harry's shoulder. 'But since you asked, like any research—slowly!'

'Yet you keep at it?' Harry persisted, thinking now of Sarah's accusation that he had simply given up on the career he'd lived for.

'I love it,' Sam said simply, and Harry felt his gut tense.

He, too, had loved his job.

Could Sarah possibly be right?

Could he continue to work in the field, even if he couldn't operate?

The realisation that the encephalitis had left him with a tremor had been shattering, especially, he realised now, because it had also left him so weak.

So he'd backed away as quickly as he could—found new challenges...

Sam was saying something about the hospital, how they intended to use his donation, but he was no longer listening, his mind too busy denying that he *could* have stayed on in his field of work.

Making excuses?

They parted on the path, but the joy he usually felt walking through the beautiful resort he'd created—an oasis of peace for people harried by the busy world—was missing.

Better to think about Sarah, about courtship—well, sex if truth be told.

And *that* thought brought a degree of discomfort somewhere inside him. She was obviously vulnerable. Nothing like the strong, focussed women he usually dallied with.

So could she handle a short affair?

Well, that was all she wanted and he could understand that now. Understand her shying away from emotional involvement, understand her fear of loss...

For her this would be a kind of trial run before moving on with life.

Which, for some unfathomable reason, made him feel even more uncomfortable.

He ignored it.

They'd keep it simple, nothing too intense—keep it light and fun, so it would be nothing more than the holiday romance, as Sarah had suggested…

Sarah sat in front of the meagre assortment of clothes in the villa wardrobe and sighed.

After the accident, she'd insisted her mother give all her clothes to charity, unable to bear the thought of wearing things that David had touched.

'So what *shall* I get you to wear?' her practical mother had asked.

Sarah hadn't been able to answer, burrowed down under the duvet, where she'd been since her release from hospital.

'I'll sort something,' her mother had said, and she had.

'I just got black and white,' she'd announced, re-turning to Sarah's flat loaded down with bags. 'Black, or white, or black and white. That way everything will go with everything else and you won't have to make choices.'

After a week of asking what Sarah might fancy for breakfast, her mother had realised her daughter couldn't make even the simplest of decisions so she'd just pro-vided a variety of meals, most of which had remained, at best, half-eaten.

Hence the poor selection of clothes Sarah still owned—black, white or black and white!

For the first time since the accident she longed for colour—for a bright emerald scarf or a red shirt…

'Nonsense,' she muttered to herself. 'You're going down there for—well, for sex, to put it bluntly. The holiday romance thing was just a way of making it sound better. As if it matters what you wear!'

She pulled a black shirt out of the cupboard—soft and silky, it felt wonderful against her skin, and even without an emerald scarf it *did* suit her colouring.

Loose white linen trousers came out next. They looked good with the shirt—they'd do.

She waved a mascara brush at her eyelashes, a touch of blusher on her cheeks, and added lipstick—bright red.

That was something she hadn't given up, defiantly sticking to the same brand and colour because someone had once told her redheads shouldn't wear red lipstick.

David had laughed and dared her to wear it always—so she did.

Oh, David, is this okay?

Stupid question! He'd be jealous as hell, but beyond that he'd probably understand that it was the next part of moving on and he'd pat her shoulder and tell her to go for it.

Pushing David very firmly to the back of her mind, she picked up her beach bag, threw a hairbrush, the lipstick and her phone into it, took a final look at herself in the mirror and headed out, her heart thudding so hard it was a wonder it wasn't bursting out of her chest.

She slipped down across the airstrip and into the shadows at the gate to the resort. During the rebuilding, the gate had been guarded but the area was now open to hospital staff either using the laboratories or deciding to get a meal in the small restaurant near the kitchens.

Sarah smiled to herself.

Restaurant meals prepared by Harry's 'minions'!

As she walked down towards his bure she felt a sense

of peace—serenity—wrap around her, and could understand why people in stressful jobs or those in the public eye would enjoy the resort.

Here they could be totally private, each bure carefully concealed in a bountiful display of tropical plants.

And right at the end, Harry's bure. He had apparently sensed her approach for he was out his door and walking towards her, taking her hands in his, looking her up and down, nodding.

'Very stylish!' he said, then, as if they'd been lifelong friends, he kissed her on the cheek.

'Come in.'

Come into my parlour, said the spider to the fly! For the first time since she'd agreed to dinner, Sarah felt a shiver of apprehension.

Or was it doubt?

Was she ready for this?

She shook it off. Of course she was, and, anyway, it wasn't as if he was going to rip her clothes off right then and there, and she could leave at any time.

He had lights burning on the deck outside, some kind of scented oil throwing flames towards the sky and casting shadows on the greenery around them.

Inside the lights had been dimmed and soft music played, music that she didn't recognise but that was soothing to her suddenly tightened nerves.

A platter of fruit, cheese and biscuits had been set on a low table in front of a divan—*the* jug, water beading on its sides, stood beside the platter.

'I do have wine,' he said, 'but try this juice first. It is a mix of pomegranate and rosewater, my mother's special recipe.'

'No wine, thanks,' Sarah said. 'I don't drink much

and never when I'm on the island. Who knows when I'll get a call to the hospital?'

'Do you get many night calls?' Harry asked as he waited for her to be seated, then poured a long glass of the brightly coloured juice, adding ice blocks from a matching bucket beside the jug.

'Very rarely, but I'd hate to get one and find I couldn't operate.'

The words were no sooner out than she regretted them. Harry couldn't operate and she could only imagine the loss that must've been to him.

But he said nothing, pouring himself a juice, settling beside her on the divan, and raising his glass.

'To no callouts tonight,' he said, the words and the slight huskiness of his voice causing a shiver to run down Sarah's spine.

She clicked glasses with him and for the first time actually noticed the slight tremor in his hand.

She wanted to touch it, to set down their glasses and hold it in both of her hands, not exactly regulation behaviour for someone embarking on an uncomplicated holiday romance.

Except she'd told him about David and the baby, so couldn't she…?

She did put down her drink, and took his hand in both of hers.

'I imagine your loss was probably as bad as mine. I lost beloved people, but you lost your life's work.'

She looked into his eyes, leaning forward to kiss him lightly on the lips.

'I *do* apologise for what I said! Was it only yesterday?'

'Yesterday or a lifetime ago,' he said quietly, retrieving his hand and using it to touch her cheek. 'But to-night is about new beginnings, not the past, so raise your drink in a toast.'

He waited until she'd lifted her glass.

'To us and our fling. May the memories we make here on Wildfire help draw a curtain across the past.'

Sarah raised her glass to touch his, and as he clinked he added, 'We're big on curtains in my country, I think because we were nomadic people originally and lived in tents, divided, to a certain extent, by curtains. And gauzy curtains soften even the harshest of landscapes.'

The curtain idea was lovely, Sarah decided as she sipped her drink, but it was forgotten as she was tantalised by the tastes she could and couldn't identify. Yes, rosewater was there—just—and the pomegranate of course, but there were hints of spices less easy to discern.

'It's beautiful,' she said, giving up on her analysis. 'A truly exquisite, refreshing drink.'

'For a truly exquisite woman.'

He raised his glass again, toasting her, and Sarah felt the blush start somewhere in her toes and race through her body to heat her throat and cheeks.

'Hardly exquisite,' she managed to mutter, then she took too big a sip of drink and promptly choked, coughing into a hastily grabbed handkerchief.

Much to her embarrassment, he slid closer, patting her gently on the back, his thigh against hers, his heat generating even more confusion in her body.

The hand that had been patting her back somehow seemed to settle around her shoulders, and although she told herself she was turning her head to thank him for the help, deep down she knew she was waiting for a kiss.

Inviting one?

Not quite, but close!

So his mouth settling on hers wasn't altogether surprising, but the effect of it galvanised nerves in parts of her body she had forgotten existed.

The kiss was gentle, explorative, persuasive rather than demanding, yet her heart rate accelerated, her breathing became unsteady, and she clung to his shoulders to anchor herself to some kind of reality.

But even that was lost when his tongue slipped inside her mouth. She gave in to desire, or need, or whatever it was that had her pulse racing and her body burning with a heat she hadn't felt for what seemed like far too long.

They were lying on the couch now, lips still joined, although his hands were inside her shirt, her fingers in his hair, holding his head, his lips, to hers with a desperation she had never felt before.

A discreet cough broke them apart.

'Minion?' she whispered, as she dragged her lips away from his, and checked the buttons on her shirt before sitting up.

'Minion!' Harry muttered back at her, hastily adjusting his own clothing.

'You stay here,' he said, as he stood up and strode to the kitchen area, where a local worker was standing with a trolley laden with silver-covered dishes, rising steam suggesting the trolley was well heated.

Harry spoke quietly to the man, who disappeared through a rear door, while the man she'd been so busy kissing on the couch pushed the trolley towards her.

She studied him, this man she'd just been kissing,

trying to work out how and why she'd felt such a strong attraction to him.

Yes, he was good-looking—strongly moulded features, clear olive skin, dark eyebrows arched above his surprising grey eyes. But there was something else that drew her to him.

Then his wry shrug, and his muttered 'Jungle drums beating wildly now' gave her at least part of the answer. As well as being possibly the sexiest man alive, he was thoughtful and considerate, worried how gossip might affect her.

'Not to worry,' she assured him. 'It's time the islands had something new to talk about. Your friend Luke's romance with Anahera had them buzzing for a while, but it's old news now.'

He pushed the trolley over to a table already set for two, before turning around to face her, the mobile eyebrow raised.

'Does it really not bother you?' he asked.

'Not at all,' she said, then she smiled as she realised just how true the words were.

Whether it was the appeal of this man, or that the healing process was nearly complete, she didn't know, but something, probably a combination of both, had released her spirit and reawakened not only a need to live but an almost urgent desire to live life to the full.

A brief affair was just what she needed, the first step in the discovery of the new Sarah Watson.

She stood up from the couch and crossed to the table, pausing to lift the lids off some of the dishes, sniffing the delicious aromas with renewed appreciation of good food.

'Thank you,' she said to Harry as she took her seat.

The bemused look on his face made her want to explain.

'For bringing me back to life,' she said. 'For reminding me of simple pleasures like a great meal or a really, really good kiss.'

The candlelit gloom made it difficult to be sure, but she was almost sure he blushed...

She was glowing, and more beautiful than any woman he had ever seen.

Surely one hot kiss couldn't have caused the transformation but, whatever it was, he hoped it stayed. Sitting there at the table, in her prim black blouse with the top button undone—had he done that?—revealing just a hint of shadowy cleavage, she was so enticing he doubted he'd be able to eat.

But he was the host so he lifted the first covered dish from the trolley and placed it on the table in front of them.

'The chef seems to have provided for all tastes. Do you like oysters? He's done Kilpatrick and Mornay and, on a special dish of ice, just natural ones. *Do* you like oysters?'

She smiled and his heart jolted in his chest.

'I could force some down,' she responded, 'although only for the zinc, of course.'

The teasing suggestion of the supposed aphrodisiac properties of the shellfish hung in the air between them.

Using the tongs provided, she selected half a dozen differently prepared shellfish for her plate.

'For the zinc, of course,' he agreed, but although he loved oysters he was far too mesmerised by the crispy, pancetta-topped Kilpatrick disappearing between her pale lips to serve some for himself.

'Here,' she said kindly. 'Try a Mornay.'

She held the fork towards him and he leaned forward to let her slide it into his mouth.

He was bewitched!

Incapable of doing anything more than sit in dumb silence, watching as she ate another one then offered the next to him.

He had to get real here, to take control. He was the host!

'More?' Sarah asked softly, and he ignored the innuendo in her words and placed the platter of oysters on the table between them.

And to show he was in control, he lifted one on his fork and offered it to her, his senses on overdrive as she opened her slightly kiss-roughened lips and sucked it from the fork.

So dinner became a prelude—a long, teasing period of foreplay—as they ate the oysters, crayfish and salad, then fed each other some kind of coconut mousse, as delightful as any dessert he'd ever tasted.

Or was it the company that made it so special?

She was leaning back in her chair, this red-headed woman he'd kind of pursued across the world, looking rosily replete and so damned beddable he had to keep reminding himself not to rush things.

'So?' she said finally, and although she managed a very small smile he could almost feel her tension across the table.

He rose and took her hand, leading her back to the divan.

'We could just chat for a while then say goodnight, and I'd drive you up to your villa...'

'Or?'

Her smile was a little stronger this time, and her green eyes glittered in the candlelit room.

'Or I could kiss you like this,' he responded, sitting down beside her and demonstrating gently.

'Or like this!'

The kiss deepened, and now she was kissing him back, inviting him into her coconut-sweet mouth, her tongue teasing at his, her hands sliding underneath the back of his shirt, touching his skin so lightly he was almost sure he moaned.

Or someone had.

His body was so aroused it was only a matter of time before their movement on the narrow divan made her fully aware of it.

'Bed?' he whispered into her mouth.

'Bed!' she responded, firmly enough to excite him even further.

He quelled a mad urge to lift her into his arms and make a dash for the bedroom.

Except he'd probably drop her! He might think he was fighting fit, but, as Luke had warned, it could take years before he fully regained the strength and mobility he'd lost in the fight for his life.

He drew her close again, and somehow, still kissing, they made a less dramatic move into the bedroom.

Where she stiffened in his arms and he realised just how big a step this was for her. He'd lost a bit of strength and the ability to do the one job he'd excelled at, the job he'd loved, while she'd lost the man she loved and a child she'd have been expecting to welcome into their family.

He eased away and took her face between the palms of his hands, looking into her eyes, at her reddened, swollen lips, remembering the taste. No, this was about her.

'We can stop right here if you like,' he told her.

And for a moment she hesitated. Then the glowing smile returned.

'And miss a night of our very short fling?' The smile widened, and he found himself wanting to watch that smile forever.

As if!

Sarah pressed her body against his, feeling his reaction to her teasing, hearing his growl as he plundered her mouth once again, backing her towards the bed while his hands roved at will over her body.

And her body responded to every move he made, so by the time he'd manoeuvred her onto the bed and was slowly undoing the buttons on her shirt she was trembling and helpless, her fingers touching his face, his hair, his chest, almost begging him to take her but lacking the words after so long a time.

And probably because he wasn't David?

A new love, even for a brief affair, needed new words, new language—language she hadn't yet learned.

Then, suddenly, words were not required. Instinct and need and want and desire all took over and although the first time was too frantic, too mind-blowing in its intensity, the second time, when their bodies had lain close and probably spoken a secret language to each

other, was slow, and languorous, and so intensely ful-
filling she clung to Harry, like a limpet to a rock, remembering the pleasure of maleness—the strength and
sinewy toughness that differentiated men from women.

'Tomorrow?' he murmured in her ear, as they lay,
spent and sweaty, once again. 'If you like, we could
take the resort boat out and snorkel along the edge of
the reef. It's another world of beauty out there.'

'Tomorrow,' she whispered back, 'I have a day of extremely unromantic and unbeautiful endoscopies to do,
and the day after that, if I remember rightly, a double
hernia op and a breast lumpectomy.'

'Ouch!'

He shuddered as she nipped her fingers on his nipple,
although earlier it had excited him.

'It's a holiday romance without the *holiday* part, remember?' she said, easing away from the enticing maleness in the bed, knowing she had to get back up to the
villa for the little that remained of the night. 'But I'm
here to work, so daytime canoodling is out.'

'Canoodling—what a great word. Is that what we've
been doing?'

'It is indeed,' she said quietly, standing up now,
searching around for clothes.

It had been David's word and although she felt no
guilt, the memory somehow brought him closer.

'Do you have to go?'

He was sitting on the bed, this Sheikh Rahman al-
Taraq, his lower body covered by a rumpled sheet, his
chest bare and smooth, slightly muscled beneath the
skin, the smile that had accompanied his question so
beguiling she almost slid back in beside him.

Almost!

'And wander back home at dawn with the eyes of the entire island on me?' she asked. 'I don't think so.'

'Then I'll drive you back.'

He was out of bed in one lithe movement and she almost gasped at her body's reaction to this naked male— this magnificent naked male.

'You d-don't have to drive me.' She stuttered out the words, aware that one touch or, worse, a goodnight kiss would have her back in bed with him in less time than it took for a single drumbeat, let alone a chorus of them.

He had things to do!

He'd told himself, when he'd made this mad dash across the world to a very small Pacific island to see again the woman with the red hair, that with the marvels of the internet he could work from anywhere.

But that had been before just one night with that same woman had blown his mind.

Now every time he closed his eyes he saw an image of her milk-white skin, the teasing smile, and long, slim arms and legs, and full breasts, and—

Open your eyes and do some work!

But although the voice he used with himself was stern, himself wasn't obeying, seeing Sarah now even when his eyes were open.

He'd go for a walk, clear his head, or go up to the research station to see what was happening there.

Or he could take the resort helicopter over to one of the uninhabited islands and gather some of the bark and leaves Sam needed for his research into M'Langi tea.

Or just take a long, cold, shower…

* * *

Sarah worked slowly and carefully, aware that any deviation in her concentration could have, well, not fatal but nasty results.

And there were so many new tracks to follow in her head that a deviation would be easy.

So she concentrated even more than usual, calling out results to Caroline, who was note-taking, although the new machine she'd bought for Wildfire computed the results.

Somehow, seeing them on paper made diagnosis easier for Sarah, and her assurances to patients that all was clear were far more heartfelt and meaningful.

Another patient was wheeled out to the top ward, today being used as a recovery room. Hettie held sway in there, keeping an eye on all the patients as they woke from their mild anaesthesia, helping them dress, then offering juice or cups of tea. Vailea, the hospital housekeeper, made sure there was a steady supply of both, and plenty of sandwiches for people who'd been nil by mouth for at least twelve hours.

The day wore on, finally finishing, and Sarah stripped off in the washroom and turned the shower to very hot. That way, if Hettie or Caroline happened to come in while she was dressing, they might think the red marks left on her body by the adventures of the previous night were from the water, nothing else.

Not that either of them came in, so Sarah dressed in the clothes she'd hastily pulled on that morning—for some reason all black—and headed to the small office to write up her notes.

The sun was almost setting, and she wasn't on the

beach. They'd made no arrangements, she and Harry, but would he look for her there?

Think she was avoiding him?

She shook her head and sighed.

Fancy complicating her life like this, even if it was only a holiday romance.

But would she not have done it to avoid complication?

No way!

Her body tingled in secret places even as she sat in Sam's chair and pulled up the information she needed from the computer.

Tingled even more when she heard his voice.

His voice!

'Anyone need a hand, someone to stand in while someone takes a break?' he was saying.

A gust of laughter from Keanu confirmed what they both already knew—jungle drums!

'You don't need an excuse to see our Sarah,' Keanu said. 'She's in the boss's office, writing up her notes. But before you interrupt her, will you take a look at an X-ray we've just done? For some reason the pictures aren't coming through from the machine as clearly as we'd like—we've an expert coming out next week to fix it. It's a little boy with an injured arm, and Sam and I both think greenstick fracture, but another pair of eyes on it would be good.'

Aware in every nerve in her body that they'd have to walk past Sam's office to get to X-Ray, Sarah held her breath, though obviously the X-ray had been taken to Harry, wherever he was out the front—maybe outside—as the murmur of their voices had grown softer.

A brief affair, she reminded herself, but her ears strained to hear his voice again, and her body continued to misbehave.

Much as he'd have loved to spend more time with her, Harry realised that a woman as dedicated as Sarah wasn't going allow herself to be distracted from her work. So he'd learned to live with her absence during the day.

He would drift up to the hospital most days, hoping to catch a glimpse of her, hear her voice, accepting the inevitable on the majority of days when it was nothing more than exercise and a time to chat with the other staff.

But late afternoons and evenings were theirs. They'd meet on the beach at sunset, swim together in the placid waters of the lagoon, then, now that the tides were kinder in the late afternoons, walk around the rock fall to his bure.

There, they'd shower, where the simple action of soaping her back had become an erotic pleasure that invariably led further. Then they'd dress and sip their juice on the deck outside until the stars were out and their dinner had been delivered.

The second night, they hadn't eaten until midnight, when hunger had forced them out of bed.

But today was the last day—the final evening of their time together lay ahead.

The thought of never seeing her again, except perhaps occasionally if their visits to Wildfire coincided, made his gut ache, but he was a man with his life in tatters; a man with family responsibilities tugging at him;

a man who could see no fixed future even for himself, let alone for anyone else.

And Sarah deserved someone better. She would never be over the losses in her life, but now that she was moving on, she deserved the best.

'Are you all right? When you didn't arrive on the beach, I—'

But he could see what she'd thought. She was breathless, her skin sheened with perspiration. She'd run from the beach to the bure thinking what? That he'd collapsed? That the encephalitis that had done so much damage to him had returned?

Not that it did, but he did suffer periodic weakness and he remembered confessing that to her.

He held out his arms and she came into them.

'I hadn't realised it was so late,' he said. 'I was thinking how much I didn't want to say goodbye.'

She pulled him closer and held him tightly.

'A fling,' she reminded him. 'It's been fun and so very good for me I cannot thank you enough, but we've still got tonight.'

'We've still got tonight,' he echoed, but as he began to unbutton her shirt he heard the helicopter take off, and a sense of foreboding made his fingers shake more than normal...

They were out on the deck, swinging lazily in a double hammock, bodies tangled together, and suddenly she wanted to know more about him and about the land where even the fountains were rose-scented.

'Tell me about your home.'

Had the fact that it was their last night together prompted the question?

Who knew? But now he was talking, his voice deep with the love he obviously felt for his homeland.

'At night in the desert the stars seem so close you could reach out and pluck a handful of them from the sky to keep in your pocket for a dark night, or to lay at the feet of a woman as homage to her beauty.'

Would you gather stars for me? Sarah wanted to ask, then reminded herself it was a holiday romance and the holiday ended tonight.

'And the sand stretches as far as the eyes can see, right up to the red and gold mountains, waving dunes of it, tempting the unwary to cross just one more hill. It is a barren beauty but I can imagine nothing more beautiful.'

Sarah moved closer, snuggling up to him.

'More,' she demanded. 'The sand, tell me about the sand.'

She felt his smile against her cheek.

'It is soft and fine, and runs through the fingers like the most expensive silk. Warm to the touch—well, too hot to touch at times, but in the shadows it will warm you, provide a bed for you, and weave itself into your life.'

And she would never see this beauty, feel the fineness of this sand—what lay between them would be memories, and on her part gratitude for his help in moving on in her life.

But was that enough?

Was that all it could be?

Of course it was, it had to be. A fling with Harry was one thing, but Sheikh Rahman al-Taraq had responsibilities to his family, to a tradition that stretched, she'd realised from snippets of conversation, back almost to the beginning of time itself.

And he also had, she remembered, a woman pledged to marry him—a woman chosen, he'd said one night, by his family—his mother. It was the way things were always done.

He was easing away from her, as if aware of her thoughts, but apparently it was hunger driving him.

'Food has yet again miraculously appeared,' he told her, holding the hammock steady as he climbed off it. 'My traditional food tonight, but little bits and pieces of it, like Spanish tapas. Do you want to sit at the table out here to eat it?'

Sarah swallowed the lump of melancholy that had formed in her throat and agreed that sitting at a table to eat was probably more sensible than handling food of any kind in a hammock.

He helped her out, held her to steady her—or perhaps just to hold her—then took her hand and led her to the small table where a platter of delicacies had miraculously appeared.

A round silver tray held myriad little dishes while a second platter had a variety of flatbreads, some thick and crusty, some wafer thin.

'Sit and taste!' Harry told her. 'The smaller, inner dishes are sauces of various kinds. You can try them by dipping bread in them, or perhaps pick up a *kibbeh*...' he lifted a small, round ball in his fingers '...and dip it in here like this.'

And he held it to her lips, his fingers trembling slightly—but, then, so were her lips and all of the rest of her body.

Whatever it was, it was delicious, a crusty outside protecting something soft and delicious—

'Eggplant?'

Harry nodded, then chose a piece of flatbread, dipping it into a steaming dish of...who knew?

'This is one of my favourites. It is *mujadara* with meat and pine nuts.'

He offered her a bite and a host of flavours she could only guess at hit her tastebuds.

'Wow!'

Harry smiled.

'Now you know how to eat our food, you must help yourself. Fingers and bread are our cutlery.'

How could the sound of a man's voice speaking about cutlery make her bones melt?

To distract herself, Sarah leaned forward and selected a small red pepper stuffed with who knew what.

'Shrimp!' she said, as once again an explosion of taste filled her mouth.

It was a culinary exploration, and with Harry's thigh tight against hers as she tried the different delights, braving all the sauces eventually, it became again a kind of foreplay.

'There are sweets,' he said, when she finally sank back, replete, against the back of the divan.

Sarah shook her head.

'If I eat again this week I'll be a pig,' she complained.

'So, we walk it off? A walk on my beach instead of yours? A *short* walk!'

He was prolonging this, their last night together, and Sarah understood, even agreed.

So they walked together past the long infinity pool

at the edge of the resort gardens and onto the private beach.

'Your stars can't be much brighter than these,' Sarah told him, waving her arms towards a heaven alight with brightness.

'Don't you believe it,' he said, turning to walk back along the beach to the bure.

Sarah opened her mouth to say she'd have to see it to believe it, then closed it again.

Theirs was a brief affair, a fling—it began and ended right here on Wildfire.

Harry held Sarah tightly against his body, his mouth opening to say, *You must come and see them*, then closing again. Remembering their decision that it would be a fling, and also the complications of his life back home.

He knew of the young woman his parents had arranged for him to marry. Had even mentioned her existence to Sarah. The chosen one was everything a man could want in a wife—beautiful, well educated, a far-removed cousin in the strange marital dance of alliances the royal family had practised for centuries.

The perfect match for a ruler!

Except he didn't wanted to rule.

His brother would be better, fairer, more involved with the people.

But the woman had been chosen. She would be expecting to marry him. To let her and both their families down would be unthinkable.

So this romance would end with this last night…

CHAPTER FOUR

'SARAH, ARE YOU down here somewhere?'

Sarah broke away from him and hurried towards Caroline.

'We tried to get you on your phone, then at Harry's. I'm so sorry, Sarah, but we've brought in a baby from one of the outer islands. Will you look at him?'

Sarah turned back towards him.

'I'm sorry,' she said. 'I have to go.'

And she hurried with Caroline along by the pool, through the quiet gardens of the resort and, presumably, up to the hospital.

Although he'd wanted to go with them, Harry knew it wasn't his place. Besides, hadn't he set aside his medical career, refusing to consider practising general medicine, which would have been more or less possible with the tremor in his hand?

So that was it!

The end of an idyll!

Maybe not!

The recent collapse of the mine having damaged the extensions to the airstrip so his jet couldn't land here, it meant they'd both be on the same plane back to Cairns in the morning...

Then he laughed at the thought!

As if anything could happen on the local, gossipy plane that was more like a holiday coach jaunt than an international flight.

No, the flight would just be something to be endured, torture, really, if that was the last he'd see of Sarah.

He wandered back to his bure, kicking at the rough coral sand, remembering other sand, his sand.

Maybe it was time he went home...

His phone was ringing as he entered the bure and for a moment he was tempted to ignore it. But something about the insistent tone made him pick up.

'Harry, I'm at the hospital. I need you!'

The urgency in Sarah's voice rang in his ears as he drove the little cart as fast as it would go up towards the hospital. Thankfully no one was around, although the privacy he'd built into the place meant you rarely met with other guests and all the staff should be home in their beds by now.

Lights were dim in the ward side but burning brightly in the small ER room and farther on in Theatre.

Sarah was waiting for him, her usual black and white replaced by theatre scrubs.

'There's a baby boy, born thirteen days ago on one of the outer islands. His mother has reported no bowel movements since birth and although he appeared to be feeding normally, he's had a lot of projectile vomiting.'

'Pyloric stenosis?' Harry asked.

Sarah nodded, her green eyes meeting his.

Pleading?

'Harry, he's badly dehydrated and Sam's working on his electrolyte balance and correcting his fluid balance, but it's there, the little olive you can feel on palpation.

They called me in—they often do if I'm here and it's a child, because I do have a fair bit of paediatric experience—but he needs an op. Now! Not after the eight hours that it would take for someone to fly over, pick him up and fly him back to Cairns.'

She paused and he wondered if she could possibly be going to ask him to operate.

On a newborn when his hand trembled?

Impossible!

'I've never operated on a child so young,' she said, hurrying on as he thought, here goes, 'so I wondered if you'd guide me through it? Stand beside me and be my brain telling my hands what to do?'

'Be your brain telling your hands what to do?'

She couldn't be serious.

'Yes, it will work, I know it will. You must have done the operation a hundred times—well, a dozen at least—so what difference will it be if it is your brain telling *my* hands what to do instead of your hands, if you know what I mean?'

The words had come out in a rush, out of the lips he'd kissed only hours earlier, but the idea was ridiculous.

Impossible!

'Please, Harry!'

Lips and green eyes pleading now.

'Just take a look at him, see how urgently he needs this op.'

Harry closed his eyes and wondered if prayer would help.

He'd left this all behind, put it away from him, lived from day to day for a long time, with the loss of something he'd set his heart and soul on doing.

Forever!

But now he was healing, getting over that loss. Wouldn't this drag him back into that time?

He looked at the woman in front of him, the woman he'd held in his arms, had kissed, had made passionate love to, and—

'We can't guarantee it would work,' he said, and knew it for a pitiful excuse.

Sarah must have known it, too, for she just waited.

'He'll need a nasogastric tube for continuous gastric lavage,' he said, and the woman in front of him positively glowed.

'Oh, Harry,' she murmured, then she became the total professional he had already seen she was. 'Come on, let's get you gowned then see our patient. Ben's okay with the anaesthetic—he did a big stint in paediatric surgery before he decided to become a writer and needed something less full time.'

Ben was a writer?

Harry shook his head. That was *so* insignificant, yet it had caught his attention in the maelstrom of emotions he was feeling as he followed Sarah down the corridor.

She could do this! Sarah told herself as she led Harry to the theatre.

With one of the world's best paediatric surgeons there to guide her, she could do this.

It would be like her first surgery experience again, only this time the guiding voice would be Harry's, not some older unknown surgeon, and her hands would be steady on the instruments.

No way could she let Harry or the baby down by being hesitant or unsure.

She turned around at the door into the changing room

and smiled at the man she'd probably pressured into helping her.

Rahman al-Taraq, his name at the top of innumerable papers on paediatric surgery, considered among the top ten in the world.

Until…

She left him to change and returned to the theatre, stopping at the door to tuck her hair into a cap, pull on a sterile apron, new booties, then went to the wash basin, scrubbing carefully—newborns were so fragile—gloving up and moving to the middle of the room, where Sam and Ben stood beside the tiny baby boy, Hettie standing behind Sam, Caroline near Ben.

Waiting…

'Will he do it?' Sam asked.

Sarah nodded.

'He's changing now.'

She didn't add *I hope it works* because these people, these friends who'd helped put her life back together, were already worried enough, without her dumping any doubts on them.

Harry came in and her heart skipped a beat.

It shouldn't be doing that when it was just a passing fling.

Neither could she have it misbehaving during the operation. Little Teo was far too important for that.

Harry moved towards the operating table, his focus on the patient lying there, his eyes taped shut, wires and tubes already attached to him, overwhelming the little body.

A trolley beside the operating table held everything Sarah had felt they would need, but Harry checked it anyway.

Already gloved, he touched the child with gentle fingers, palpating his stomach, feeling the little lump that was proof that his stomach was blocked where it should empty into the intestines, and the operation was a necessity.

'So!'

He looked around at the assembled crew.

'Not my usual team but I couldn't ask for better,' he said, waving Sarah towards him.

He looked at Ben.

'You ready?'

Ben nodded and injected the anaesthetic into a tube already in place.

'You happy with the nasogastric tube, Sam?'

'It's secure and we've a gentle suction attached to it.'

'So, let's go!'

He smiled at Sarah as he said it, and for all his voice fired every nerve in her body, she set everything else aside and focussed on the little boy they needed to save.

Praying this would work, Harry began.

'Three-centimetre incision just below the right rib cage, careful of the liver, see…'

Sam was cauterising the small blood vessels, and as Harry talked he could watch Sarah's steady gloved hands following his instructions. The teacher in him kept coming out as he explained things to the others— how gentle traction with a damp sponge just here— Hettie followed that order—could bring a curve to the stomach to allow best access to the pylorus.

Each step seemed to take forever, but with such a tiny baby there were so many things that could go wrong.

Cutting too deep could be as disastrous as not cutting deeply enough.

Sarah followed his instructions with neat, sure movements, finding the side of the pylorus that lacked blood supply, placing the longitudinal cut along the wall of the tiny bead, cutting into the outer skin but not going deep enough to do any damage to the inner walls.

'Now, gently spread the lips of the cut apart until the mucosa puffs up—there, you've got it. Excellent. Now, who has the slow absorbable sutures? I use a running stitch but you can use interrupted ones.'

He watched as, with more confidence now, Sarah sewed up the layers of tissue and muscle through which she'd cut, finally asking Sam to add butterfly closures across the wound to ensure its closure.

Harry was uncertain what he felt as he left the theatre, Sarah staying on as if unwilling to leave their fragile patient.

Satisfaction, certainly, but…

Was Sarah right?

Did he have something to offer to paediatric surgery, even if he couldn't operate?

Probably, but surely it would never be enough.

No, what he was feeling must be nostalgia. He had new interests, more than enough to keep him busy, and maybe, just maybe, he could fall in line with his family's wishes and go home to learn at least something of his country's politics.

Yet the words Sarah had thrown at him that night still rankled.

And the fact that their last night together—the one

night he'd known she'd stay with him—had been cut so short rankled, as well.

How selfish was that!

Of course Sarah would want to stay with the baby.

Hadn't he needed to watch over babies he'd operated on?

They'd always seemed too fragile for the indignities he'd made them suffer, too small for him to be invading their bodies.

The dull ache of all he'd lost returned, and he realised it was the first time since he and Sarah had made love that he'd felt what had been an ever-present pain before.

Because he'd known their time together would be so short?

Surely not!

Sarah wasn't sure why she'd stayed. There were plenty of more than competent people watching over little Teo, yet somehow she couldn't leave the quiet room where machines still helped him breathe, and wires taped to his chest showed all his vital signs on the monitor above his bed.

Yet still she had to stay, as if in apology to the little one whose body she'd invaded.

She thought of Harry, wondered if he'd be expecting her, yet somehow knew he'd understand her needing to be here.

So, tomorrow on the flight back to Cairns would be their last time together. She had a few days off then a flight to Emerald in Central Queensland, a week of surgery there, patients brought in from hundreds of miles around the large country town.

While Harry, well, she'd seen the blue-and-gold-painted executive jet on the tarmac at Cairns airport from time to time. It matched the colours of the little helicopter that sat on the tarmac here at Wildfire, always ready to take visitors on a trip to one of the outer islands, or simply a flight over the marvels of the reef that surrounded M'Langi.

Harry would be whisked away in his pretty plane to places she could only imagine. Not back to the desert with its silken sands but probably to Africa to check up on his projects there, or to South-East Asia to see for himself how his mosquito eradication programme was progressing.

Harry!

Weird how they'd started out hurting each other, then—

Well, all holiday romances must come to an end.

'How's our patient?' Harry asked when Sarah appeared at the airstrip while the place was still being unloaded.

She flashed a radiant smile that hit him in the gut.

'Brilliant!' she said. 'The staff know how to treat him, and they're the best, so he'll be fine.'

Now beneath the happiness he saw her exhaustion.

'You haven't slept,' he said, and heard an edge of what couldn't possibly be anger in his voice. As if her sleep—or lack of it—was any of his business.

'I usually sleep on the plane,' she said. 'And I've a few days off to catch up anyway.'

It shouldn't be like this. Harry's mind, or maybe some other part of him, was protesting. This shouldn't be how it ended, polite nothings on an airstrip.

But what else was there?

The two of them in a bubble of—what, emotion?—

amongst the bustle of people coming and going. All words said, their time together was already becoming nothing more than a memory.

'Hi!'

The bubble burst as Ben arrived, a wodge of papers stuck untidily under one arm, a duffle bag in the other.

'Maybe I won't be sleeping on the plane,' Sarah said, smiling at the new arrival and taking the papers from under his arm.

'Did you finish this last night?' she asked Ben, who nodded happily, although he looked even more tired than Sarah.

'I'm his first reader,' Sarah explained, turning back to Harry, explaining politely, as if this was all perfectly normal.

Wasn't her body shouting that it hadn't had enough?

Weren't her fingers longing to touch his shoulder, his cheek, perhaps run a thumb across his lips?

How could she just stand there chatting about Ben's latest book, which she apparently was going to read on the plane? Now even sitting next to her was probably out of the question.

He had obviously been mad to start something he couldn't finish properly. To begin an affair that couldn't possibly come to its natural conclusion.

Holiday romance, indeed!

Yet Sarah seemed unfazed. Tired, yes, but remarkably at ease, as if their few nights together were already forgotten. As if the passion with which she'd kissed him could be turned off so easily.

Like flicking a switch!

Whereas he just wanted to rip off all her clothes—

or maybe undress her slowly—and finish what they'd started in a way more suited to a holiday romance...

Sarah hugged the mess of papers that was Ben's latest masterpiece to her chest, thankful it would excuse her from sitting next to Harry on the flight back. Ben would claim the seat next to her—previous experience told her that. He'd want to know, every ten minutes, what she thought of it so far...

But sitting next to Harry would have been agony. Already she was having trouble controlling fingers that wanted to stroke his cheek, hands that wanted to rest lightly on the back of his waist, or on his neck, or head, or, really, anywhere at all on Harry.

She wanted the licence her fingers and hands had had to roam his body, learning him by touch, while other senses devoured him, inhaling the scent of him, thrilling to the roughness in his deep voice when he made love, seeing the light in his grey eyes when she made him laugh.

Oh, Harry...

She looked his way, caught his eyes on her, and knew he, too, felt the urge to touch.

It was because their last night together had been cut short that their little romance felt unfinished. It had to be that, for her body to be wanting him so badly.

Thank heaven for Ben.

Sitting next to Harry for four hours and *not* ripping off his clothes would have been unbearable.

'Okay, folks, remember we go through customs when we land, so leave anything illegal here on the island.'

The pilot and co-pilot were ones Sarah had flown with before, and the co-pilot, in charge of loading, always began the flight the same way. At the top of the steps leading into the plane one of the two cabin staff waited, a list in his hand.

Sarah smiled to herself. The flight crew would all know who was going to be on the plane and also which of the various islanders could cause problems, often trying to smuggle a live chicken or even a piglet on board, to be part of a celebration feast with their family in Australia.

Sarah lifted her bag then felt the weight go from her hand, fingers brushing hers, sending a shock along her nerves.

Hadn't she just put all thoughts of touching Harry from her mind? Cooled down her over-active imagination and her body?

And told herself to think ahead, not backwards? It was finished, done, nothing more than they'd intended it to be—a holiday romance...

'I can carry it!' she snapped, disturbed by that shock wave when everything between them was over.

'Fight me for it?' he suggested, in the husky voice he used in bed, the same husky voice that fired her entire body with waves of heat and desire.

She shrugged but kept her fingers on the handle.

How weak are you, Sarah Watson, to be pretend holding hands when the holiday is over?

The seemingly never-ending flight finally ended, the plane touching lightly down in Cairns, releasing Sarah from the agony of knowing Harry was directly behind her, his body bombarding hers with subliminal messages as she battled to read Ben's book.

Harry stood up to lift her bag from the overhead

compartment, then quelled her protest with a look as he carried both her bag and his from the plane. So they stood together in the queue for Customs, the messages no longer subliminal as their bodies touched when the new arrivals pressed forward.

Memories of other body-touching made her knees go weak, and it was only with the utmost resolution that she shut down the memories.

She was saying goodbye to this man, and had to be cool, calm and clinical about it.

Deep breath!

'I don't know what to say, other than goodbye,' Sarah murmured to him, knowing her voice would be lost in the hubbub and only Harry would hear it. 'And to say thank you. It was really, really special to me and I'll always remember our time together.'

'Wow, that seemed to come right from the heart!' Harry muttered angrily at her. 'Did you really feel it necessary to offer polite nothings?'

'Well, what have you to say?' Sarah demanded, wondering just why this particular man could fire her temper so easily.

He didn't answer and, looking into his face, she realised he didn't know—any more than she had when she'd struggled to find words.

The tightness in her chest eased, and she touched him on the arm.

'There are no words,' she said softly, 'other than goodbye.'

'Or I might need to be in Wildfire in six weeks,' he suggested.

Sarah shook her head.

'I'm taking time off after this next trip—six weeks—

time enough to go back to England and spend some decent time with the family, rather than a rushed three-day Christmas visit.'

Although the prospect of going home no longer had the appeal and excitement that had been there when she'd booked the trip.

Damn the man, he really *had* got under her skin!

Flurried, she repeated her goodbye but more firmly this time…

Goodbye?

Harry's brain struggled to grasp the concept.

This was goodbye?

Of course it was. What had he expected her to say?

And as she'd said, what did he have to say that would be better?

He was still struggling with these thoughts when she stepped up to the arrivals desk, had her passport stamped, then lifted her bag from the floor near his feet, opened it ready for a cursory inspection, and moved through the barrier.

Getting farther and farther away from him, especially when the man stamping passports wanted to talk about his country.

Ambelia!

The word stuck in his head and a sudden rush of homesickness all but overwhelmed him.

He wouldn't go to Africa. His pilot would have to change their flight plan.

He'd go home.

And perhaps there he'd forget the woman with the vibrant red hair and slim white body who had just disappeared through a door and out of his life…

CHAPTER FIVE

IT WASN'T EXACTLY BORING, Sarah's trip west. In fact, there were some interesting patients and she liked Emerald as a town.

But something was missing and, loath as she was to admit it, she knew it was Harry's presence—Harry's lovemaking, and just Harry himself.

Stupid, really, because now that she'd rediscovered her sexual self, she could enjoy a relationship with anyone she fancied.

Providing, of course, they fancied her back.

Not that she'd be slipping straight into bed with them as she had with Harry. No, she could take her time, get to know someone, let a relationship build.

Perhaps that was why she was missing Harry—because the time they'd spent together could hardly be called a relationship. They'd done it all backwards.

Maybe, given time, she'd have got over the need to brush her fingers across his skin, or trace the tiny scar beside his ear, or stroke her hand down his firm thigh.

Got over the need to touch him at all.

'You want to come into town for a bite to eat? There's that great Indian restaurant just off the main drag.'

Ben had knocked on the door of her motel room and poked his head through the gap.

He'll want to talk about his book, Sarah thought, and shook her head, then regretted it when she saw the disappointment on his face.

But tonight she just wanted to brood.

To try to work out why a certain Rahman al-Taraq had stirred the embers of her dead emotions back to smouldering life.

In five days?

Well, less, in the end.

The attraction had begun, on her side anyway, from the moment she'd helped him from the water with the stonefish sting.

And the discomfort—the shock, really—of that slow burn through her body had made her hit out at him.

But he *was* wasted, doing what he did.

Thankfully, her mobile belted out a jaunty tune at that stage of her brooding over Harry, and a desperate search for it distracted her completely.

So when she finally found it and answered, and a deep, sultry, masculine voice said, 'Sarah, I need you,' she almost fainted on the spot.

Had she conjured him up out of her thoughts?

And was need the same as want?

But he was still talking, and she had to listen. Apparently, Harry had touched down in Ambelia to complete chaos. His youngest sister had just given birth to her first baby, and he suffered from exactly the same problem as the baby boy on Wildfire Island: pyloric stenosis.

'She wants me to do the op, Sarah, and you know I can't. But we've done it together once before and could do it again. Will you help me?'

'Oh, Harry, how can I? We're at opposite ends of the world.'

'My plane is on the way to Cairns as we speak. Will you come?'

She *had* to go!

She'd needed him and he'd come.

'Can your pilot fly into Brisbane? It's easier for me to get quickly from here to there than from here to Cairns. I've one small op in the morning, then I'll get an afternoon flight to Brisbane. Should get in around five in the afternoon.'

'He'll be waiting at the airport for you,' Harry promised.

Sarah didn't know what to say—even how to say goodbye. Not without sounding over formal, which would come across as cold.

Harry broke the silence.

'Thank you, Sarah.'

Then he was gone.

Had that really happened? Or had she imagined it?

But, no, she was still holding her mobile in her hand so she'd been talking to *someone*.

And now excitement began to build. Changing her flight was easy on the internet and she messaged Harry to let him know her flight details.

Then she sat down, ran her hands through her hair, and considered what she'd agreed to do.

Which was when the enormity of it all hit her.

She'd see Harry again, see the desert and feel the sands run through her fingers like silk. Of course, she'd have to check she could fly from there to London, and if it was summer here would it be cold in...

She dug through memories of her time with Harry but nowhere could she find the name of his country.

Back on the net, she ran a search on Rahman al-Taraq and discovered the country was Ambelia and that Harry was heir to the throne.

A sudden sadness filled her when she saw Harry still listed as a gifted and world-renowned paediatric surgeon.

She shied away from that, looking up Ambelia instead, reading that the discovery of copper as well as the ever-present oil had made the country very wealthy.

'The wealth is spread amongst the people,' the article continued, 'although many Ambelians live in traditional ways, with nomads following ancient trade routes in the desert, and fishermen using the traditional dhows to ply their trade.'

Excitement stirred, the thrill of the unknown mixing with the physical sensations she was experiencing at the thought of seeing Harry again.

It was only when he'd ended the call, heart hammering in his chest at the prospect of seeing Sarah again, that Harry realised it had a downside.

He had his own suite of rooms and his own staff in a section of the palace, but his mother would insist that Sarah stay in one of the guest suites.

On the far side of the rambling building!

And while jungle drums might be quick to pick up gossip, they were as nothing compared to the speed of palace gossip.

It came of having too many staff with too little to do, but most of them were fourth- or even fifth-generation retainers to the royal family, which made sacking any of them inconceivable.

So Sarah would be here, but not here for him—not close enough to touch, to slowly undress, to lie in his bed and make those little breathy moans when he pleasured her.

His body tightened.

There had to be a way.

But even reserving a suite for her in one of the six-star hotels was out of the question.

Hotels, too, had staff, and though he'd spent little time at home in the last years—in fact, since he'd been ten and had gone to boarding school—he was still easily recognisable...

He sighed, cursing himself for not thinking this thing through. To have her here, so close, but untouchable—

Hell and damnation, he couldn't touch her anyway. His engagement was due to be announced, already postponed because of Miryam's baby...

He had to see speak to his mother, ask her to speak to Yasmina—to explain.

Explain just what, exactly?

That a woman with whom he'd had a brief holiday romance was coming to the country and he'd like to continue their relationship?

Great thing to dump on any woman, but to someone who was related, whose family had already agreed to the marriage...

Impossible!

But it was equally impossible to marry Yasmina when he had feelings for Sarah. The exact nature of the feelings were a little confused, but they did exist...

Didn't they?

He sighed.

Even with the little he knew of Sarah, he knew she'd laugh at the situation—the two of them close but not close enough…

He gritted his teeth and messaged her the name of the acting consul in Brisbane who would meet her plane and take her to the private section of the international airport. Youssef would see her onto the Ambelia-bound jet.

Damn!

He could have flown out with the plane, met her in Australia, then at least he'd have had the ten hours' flight time to…

Make love to her?

Because that *was* all he wanted, wasn't it?

Now uncertainty raised its head, but he decided to ignore it. He had enough to do organising someone to meet Sarah at the airport, visiting Miryam at the hospital, arranging staff to be on standby for the op on his little nephew.

More than enough to do, so why was his mind stuck on seeing Sarah again?

Perhaps because she might not be quite as excited about seeing him?

A brief affair, a fling, she'd said.

Finished when their time on the island ended.

But we didn't have that final night, a pathetic voice cried in his head, and he quelled it firmly, called someone to take a message to the stables for his horse to be saddled.

He'd forget about Sarah, go for a ride and watch the sunset from his own beach—hundreds and hundreds of miles of it.

* * *

Sarah sat back in the plush leather chair in the luxury jet, playing with the buttons that made the chair lie flat or worked the small TV in front of her.

She'd been offered champagne, juice or water before the plane had even taken off, but had stuck with water, aware she could become dehydrated on the flight and wanting to arrive as alert as possible. The operation had already been delayed just getting her to Ambelia.

Ambelia—Harry's home...

Once in the air, she was fed, the spices in the food, the little dishes of sauce reminding her of her last night on the island.

That last night they were supposed to have been together.

Reminding her of their mutual desire to drain as much pleasure as possible out of it.

But that had been then and this was now, and as it had been nothing more than a brief fling, it was best to tuck it away in her memory and think of the future.

Her future!

The four years in Australia had helped her heal, but maybe it was time to think of returning home permanently. Her parents weren't getting any younger, and Australia was a long way off if she was needed urgently.

And operating on the baby had reminded her of her ambition...

She sighed and settled back into her seat, letting it recline so she could put her feet up and doze.

As if that was going to be possible, when Harry was at the end of this journey and memories of their short time together played like movies on the inside of her eyelids.

* * *

The ride had been a good idea—racing his stallion across the dunes behind the palace had been invigorating. The problem was, he shouldn't have dismounted, shouldn't have picked up a handful of sand and let it run through his fingers.

Was this to be his fate in life, that even the simplest of pleasures would remind him of Sarah?

He rode home less swiftly, and went to visit Rajah in his palatial enclosure. The big animal trumpeted softly in greeting, and not for the first time Harry wondered just how old his friend might be. He'd been born in the circus and the man who had owned him had been sure he was at least twenty when Harry's father had bought him.

Too old, the man had said, to be retrained to live in the wild. But that was thirty-five years ago.

Could elephants live into their fifties and sixties?

Rajah's trunk explored Harry's pockets, seeking a treat that he'd usually find.

'Nothing today, old boy,' Harry told him, scratching at the more tender skin behind the animal's ear. 'I'm too out of whack to have thought of it,' he continued. 'There's this woman, you see…'

And he poured out the story of Sarah, and attraction, and the frustration that lay ahead for him—perhaps for both of them—while she was a guest at the palace.

Rajah nodded wisely, but Harry knew he probably needed more than an elephant's wise nod to sort out his mind and body.

The sun was rising over a distant horizon as they came in to land at Ambelia, and Sarah stared with wonder at the world she was about to enter. There were the dunes Harry had told her of, stretching to red and golden mountains, and there was the sea, dotted with fishing boats so small they looked like toys.

The tall towers of a modern city glinted in the early morning sunlight, but it was the large walled estate beyond the city that drew her eyes. Minarets reached towards the sky, round domed buildings stood among rectangular ones, courtyards seemed to be scattered like embroidered handkerchiefs between the buildings and the whole complex within the walls was ringed with more greenery and formally laid-out gardens.

Then it was gone, the city and the old walled complex, and they were coming in smoothly to land.

Now there were no distractions.

Very soon she would be seeing Harry again.

Or maybe he'd be at the hospital with his sister and her child, and she would have to put up with the flock of butterflies dancing in her stomach for even longer.

The crew unlocked doors and a stairway slid into place, then Harry was there, right in front of her, his face tense and pale as if he, too, was feeling uncertain about this meeting.

Only it wasn't Harry, it was Rahman al-Taraq, a gold-braided circlet holding his snowy white checked head-cloth in place, more gold dribbling down the front of his immaculate white gown, tiny embroidery stitches outlining an opening in the front.

And she stared—probably open-mouthed—at the man she knew yet didn't know, then his eyes looked deep into hers and her lungs seized up.

A slight smile twitched on his lips.

'Sorry about the regalia. There was stuff I had to do on the way to the airport.'

Still trying to regain control of her lungs, and other rioting body parts, all Sarah could manage was a vague nod.

Had he read just how paralysed she was? He bent over, reaching out to undo her seatbelt, his voice shaking slightly as he said, 'Thank you for coming, Sarah,' in that deep, husky voice that played havoc in her dreams.

She had to get with it—she was here, this was Harry, they would operate on the baby and then she'd be gone.

His being dressed in his traditional garb reminded her of just how big a gulf lay between them culturally, and also reminded her he had a wife-to-be waiting somewhere in the shadows—possibly in one of the white buildings she'd seen from the plane, the ones in the walled complex.

So forget the husky voice and dreams and show some strength.

All she could muster was the smallest of smiles.

'My pleasure,' she said, as his hand took hers to help her to her feet. 'I was coming in this direction anyway,' she added, because if she didn't talk she'd forget about strength and do something stupid like throw herself into his arms. 'It's on the way home to England, more or less, so it's no trouble…'

Her voice trailed away as Harry pulled her towards him and held her in a gentle hug, then kissed her on both cheeks. She could feel his heart hammering against his ribs, probably in tune with hers, but the cabin crew was waiting for them to leave the plane, so there'd be no proper kiss.

Not in Ambelia! Not now she'd met Rahman al-Taraq and realised just how impossible this situation was.

Would there ever be a proper kiss again?

Hardly!

It had been a brief affair—they'd both understood that.

So why was her body betraying her with its heat? And, come to that, the tight grip on her hand felt like Harry's rather than Rahman's.

But this *wasn't* Harry from the resort. Here he was the ruler-in-waiting, and here he had a woman pledged to marry him and subjects who'd take a great interest in every move he made.

The robes made those facts perfectly clear.

Sarah sighed.

Unless there were very roomy linen cupboards at the hospital they might have to forget the attraction side of their relationship—put it behind them.

For the duration of her visit?

She sighed again, but softly.

In truth, it was probably forever, given his position, and the wife in waiting, and the fact that it had only ever been a holiday romance.

Warmth hit her as she exited the plane, but it was pleasant, soft and dry as it enfolded her body. She was following Harry down the steps, and he stopped at the bottom and turned to take her hand, presumably to help her make the last step safely.

His fingers gripped hers hard, and she squeezed his in return.

'This is possibly the most ridiculous mistake I've made in my entire life!' he muttered angrily. 'I must know at least twenty excellent paediatric surgeons in

London that I could have flown in, but no, I had to complicate my life—and probably yours—by demanding you.'

And Sarah smiled.

At least they were both suffering.

No matter who he was—Harry, heir, husband-to-be—it was obvious their affair felt unfinished to him, too.

Not that that was much consolation so she forgot about the man who was now striding ahead to a waiting limousine, and forced her mind to think about what lay ahead—to think about a tiny baby who needed the expertise of both of them.

'Did you sleep on the flight?' he asked abruptly, opening a rear door of the car for her.

'Most of the way,' she replied. 'I spend a lot of my time in planes far less comfortable than yours, and have learned to sleep on all of them.'

She looked directly at him, refusing to be distracted by the robes and headdress, and looking instead at his pale, hypnotic eyes and the grim set of his lips. At the tiny scar she'd traced with her fingers, and which she knew grew paler when he was stressed.

Very pale. The way it was now.

His tension was evident, but she was here to do a job, not to dally with this man, no matter how appealing more dallying might be. So right now she had to make it plain that the visit was for work.

She took a deep breath and, well, prattled...

'I think we learn to sleep at any time in any place during our training, don't you? It's probably nearly as important as learning anatomy, given the lives we lead, especially during our early days in hospitals.'

Now it wasn't just his lips that looked grim. He was positively glowering at her.

But she wasn't to be put off by a glower.

She waited until he'd stalked around the car and got in the other side behind a silent driver, then, determined to keep things as casual as possible between them, she asked, 'How's the baby? Is the op urgent? I'm confident I could go straight into Theatre, although a shower and a cup of tea would be a nice way to relax first.'

'A shower and a cup of tea?' he repeated, the disbelief in his voice so strong it was like a physical force. 'Is that all you can say?'

She turned towards him and, hoping the driver who was now concentrating on getting the vehicle through the airport traffic wouldn't see the motion, she took his nearest hand and held it in both of hers.

'What else is there to say, Harry?' she said softly. 'Or should I call you Rahman here?'

She squeezed his fingers.

'What we had was wonderful, but I know, and you know, that we can't take it further—not now you're home and definitely not here, where word of any relationship between us would get back to the woman you are going to marry and so, I'm sure, shame your family as well as hurting her.'

He bent his head, his hand still in hers, although now his fingers gripped hers as if he thought she might let his go.

'The baby,' she repeated quietly. 'Tell me about the baby. Let's concentrate on that and think about the rest later.'

He raised his head but didn't look at her.

'He's doing well. He arrived fourteen days early,

which was hardly a problem, but the stenosis wasn't picked up until the projectile vomiting started three days ago. I think the pylorus wasn't totally blocked at first. Since the diagnosis, he's been having limited amounts of parenteral nutrition, and the doctors are keeping a constant check on his electrolyte balance and hydration.'

'And his mother, your sister?'

Now he turned to look at her, and she saw the ravages that concern for his sibling and her child had left on his face.

'Miryam's been wonderful. She stays by his bedside night and day, her gloved hand through the window in the sterile crib, touching him, talking to him. Her husband is there as well, most of the time, but I've learned women are far better than men at handling things like this.'

His face lightened and he almost smiled.

'You'd have thought I'd have worked that out long ago, but until it becomes personal there are things you don't see. Miryam's husband has to leave the room to go into a corner somewhere and cry from time to time. It's the only way he can keep going for his wife and child.'

Harry squeezed her fingers, adding, 'I've felt for him—felt his tears—teared up myself. Pathetic, really.'

'Nonsense,' Sarah said, removing her hand before he broke the fingers she'd need for the operation. 'This is your family, people you love, in pain and trouble. You're entitled to get emotional about it because you're human. Miryam probably cries sometimes as well, and her husband holds her and gives her strength to continue. But, being a man, he won't let her see *his* tears in case she loses faith in his strength.'

Grey eyes studied her face for a moment, then the slightest of smiles touched his lips.

'Maybe I *was* right to call you...'

Was that a compliment? Sarah wondered, then told herself to stick to the plan—be practical, do the job, go home to England...

'We're nearly at the hospital. If you're sure you're happy to go ahead—after your shower and cup of tea—I'll let them know.'

He lifted a cell phone out his pocket and spoke words Sarah didn't understand. Soft, strange words that touched her heart, while her eyes were on the man himself, on the hand that held the phone and the fingers that had brought her body such pleasure, on the lips she'd kissed, the neck—

'They'll be ready. I didn't know what tea so they'll make a selection and you can choose.'

CHAPTER SIX

THE HOSPITAL WAS UNBELIEVABLE, reasonably new and laid out in spacious, beautifully maintained gardens. The buildings were white, two and three stories high.

'Each unit is complete,' Harry told her, as the limo pulled up at a portico entrance, 'ER, Outpatients, Radiography, Theatre and wards. There's a central pathology lab that does all the blood and culture work. This is the children's block. You can see it's built around a central courtyard. Even after generations of urbanisation, we still like to be close to the outdoors. Many family members of hospitalised children will sleep in the portico outside their relative's room.'

'So the hospital was built to accommodate families?' Sarah asked, looking around in wonder at the beautiful interior—the entrance was like that of a five-star hotel.

'Family is important to us,' Harry said, although she realised it was Rahman talking, and Harry only when he touched her lightly on the arm and added, 'I am sorry. Talk of family must be painful.'

She turned towards him, wanting to look at him, to make sure it *was* Harry under the unfamiliar clothing.

'I only lost part of my family. The rest of them helped me through, kept me going, until I ran away from their

kindness because I knew I *had* to do it myself—to put
myself back together again, possibly in a way that was
different from their expectations. Do you understand
that?"

She need not have asked, because the understanding
was there in his eyes and in the little extra pressure of
the hand that rested on her arm.

He had to stop touching her, had to take his hand off
her arm, yet how could he? A friendly touch like this
was all the contact he would be able to make with her,
surrounded as he was by the ever-present interest of the
people of his country.

He'd been away so long he attracted extra interest
wherever he went and he knew the gossip would be rife.

Was he here to stay this time?

Would he take over from his father, as had been or-
dained by his lineage?

Had he come home to be married?

It was time he produced an heir…

He guided Sarah towards the theatre area of the
building and handed her over to a young woman who
was hovering near the tea room.

'Would you show Dr Watson the bathrooms when
she finishes her tea?' he said, then weakened. 'No, don't
worry, I'll have tea with her. We can talk about the operation, then I'll show her the way to the showers.'

'How weak am I?' he said gruffly, aware his an-
noyance was with himself. 'Wanting just a few more
minutes alone with you, but not in the way I'd like to
be alone.'

Sarah turned her green eyes on him, her pain clear
to see.

'Harry, we *have* to put what happened between us in the past. You have duties to your family here, a woman expecting to marry you. We'll do the op then I'll be gone. Why torture ourselves needlessly when we know this can't go anywhere?'

The shock was like a knife going into his chest.

'But you have to see the sand—my sand—and meet Rajah. I have so much to show you—'

She lifted her hand in front of her, an obvious stop signal, and shook her head to emphasise the point.

'No, Harry,' she said softly. 'I cannot do anything with you. With a guide, perhaps, but not with you. You know as well as I do the attraction is still there and being alone together would be stupid. You have—'

Now *he* stopped *her*.

'A duty. I'm sorry, that was stupid, but...'

She poured a cup of tea, and sipped at it.

'There are too many buts, Harry. Too many ifs and buts and whys and maybes. We had fun together, shared passion for a while, but now it's back to real life for both of us.'

He felt anger flare, and wanted to rage at her, or more probably at himself. She was just too calm, talking about passion without a hint of it in her face or voice.

And hadn't it been more than that?

She finished her tea and stood up, collecting the small bag he'd carried off the plane and set beside their chairs.

'Bathroom?' she asked, and now she smiled and he was back on Wildfire, soaping her long, white back, counting down the vertebrae with his fingertips, inciting them both to—

Passion!

'This way.'

He spoke abruptly and led her out of the room, pushing open the door to the women's dressing room, calling
to someone inside to show Dr Watson where everything was kept.

'See you in Theatre?' Sarah asked, and he heard
anxiety in her voice.

Instead of calmly and quietly discussing what lay
ahead of them, he'd been fuming over her withdrawal
from him—a withdrawal he deserved. After all, *he* was
the one with commitments.

He nodded a reply then calmed himself down before
seeking out Miryam, wanting to speak to her, reassure
her, before he had to change for Theatre.

His youngest sister was in the theatre waiting room,
together with his mother, two other sisters and a horde
of aunts and cousins crammed into what he'd always
thought a reasonably sized room.

His mother seized him first.

And right at the back of the crowded room, his father, sitting in an armchair, two grandchildren on his
knee, quietly watching over his family.

'She's here, the doctor?' his mother demanded, and
Harry assured not only her but all the clamouring relations that Dr Watson had indeed arrived and would be
in Theatre within minutes.

He took Miryam's hands in his.

'I know it's hard to think so young a baby, your baby,
has to have an operation, but it is simple and Dr Watson
is an excellent surgeon. I will stand behind her and tell
her what to do. She will be my hands, so your baby's
life will be in my hands, as you wished.'

He kissed her cheek then held her close for a moment, though inwardly aware that it was his sister's insistence he operate that had brought him and Sarah together again.

Having done the same operation with Sarah once, he had known this was the safest way to proceed. Other paediatric surgeons would have their own ways of working and would not want him hovering over them. But while having Sarah close again when he'd been trying to convince himself it was all over was bad enough, having her close and untouchable was even worse.

He had to stop thinking about their relationship—or lack of it—and direct all his thoughts to what lay ahead.

Focus on his sister's baby—his nephew. This was family.

All his attention must be focussed on the baby.

He could do this, he reminded himself as he introduced Sarah to the team already in place, then stood beside her but a little behind her, to keep out of the way of people operating instruments.

He *could* do this, although as he spoke and her hands moved, he felt as if they were not two people but two parts of a whole, working in tandem, the feel of her body close to his so familiar it was like part of him, her fingers on the scalpel his as well as hers.

It was a slow and careful process. So tiny an infant had a lot of very necessary paraphernalia tucked into his little body, all of which must be kept intact.

But Sarah never lagged, never slumped or hesitated, her hands sure and steady as he told them what to do.

And when the job was done, the baby taken to Recovery, he touched Sarah on the shoulder. Her hair was hidden by the theatre cap, her face pale from the strain of the work she'd done, but to him she was as beautiful as he had ever seen her.

He couldn't let it end.

Not the way it had, and not now, with hard words between them.

Yes, it had been a fling, but there'd been something deeper between them, something he was sure Sarah felt as keenly as he did. It was up to him to give them more time together—time to look past the passion that they'd shared and maybe just a little way into the future.

Time…

'I have a few things to do,' he said, 'the family to see. Will you wait for me in the tea room?'

She looked at him as if trying to assess his reasoning, but in the end smiled and nodded.

'I could be a while,' he added.

She simply said, 'I'll wait.'

Right! Family first—reassurances for Miryam, then a quiet word with his mother. She would know the best way to go about things, and, though undoubtedly she'd be disappointed in his decision, she'd understand it was the right thing to do.

Probably!

Sarah waited in the tea room, nibbling at the delicate pastries that were brought to her, chatting to other staff who'd been in Theatre with her as they stopped for tea or coffee before heading back to whatever jobs they had to do.

They came and went through an inner door, so when the outer door opened she turned, expecting it to be Harry, feeling disappointment when she saw the traditionally dressed woman, a long black cloak covering whatever she was wearing underneath, a headscarf wrapped in some mysterious fashion around her hair.

Miryam, the baby's mother!

She moved on soundless feet across the room, sinking down beside Sarah, taking her hand.

'I must thank you for what you did today, for saving my baby. I know Rahman feels the loss of his profession very keenly, and he must have great trust in you to ask you to do it.'

Sarah, embarrassed by the praise, tried to brush it away.

'It was nothing—anyone would have done it—'

'No, not anyone. Only someone who has lost a child would understand my terror. Rahman told me of your accident. It makes your action today even braver.'

Tears were sliding down Miryam's face, and Sarah put her arm around the woman, blinking away her own tears.

'There, he'll be all right now and I would think he'll be out of Recovery very soon. You'll want to be with him, I know.'

Miryam nodded, then found a tiny scrap of lace handkerchief somewhere in her voluminous robe and wiped her eyes.

'I'll go but you will be in my heart, forever in my gratitude for what you did.'

She rose gracefully, touched Sarah on the shoulder then glided away—soundlessly again.

Sarah mopped her own eyes. The young woman's gracious words had touched her heart, and once again she wondered about her future.

Was it too late to go back—to join a paediatric surgical team and start again at the bottom to achieve that old dream?

She heard the door but no footsteps—not Harry, then—and turning saw another figure robed in black.

The grey eyes told her all she needed to know even before the woman introduced herself as Hera, Rahman's mother.

Uh-oh!

Sarah put aside the discomfort she felt at this gracious woman's presence.

'Hera is a pretty name—wasn't she a goddess in ancient times?'

Hera smiled.

'The goddess of women and marriage. Our families go back a long, long way,' she said, and although she possibly didn't mean as far back as Greek gods and goddesses, she was making a point.

A 'keep away from my son' point?

An 'I'm in charge of his marriage' point?

Sarah didn't have a clue, although she didn't feel any animosity as the woman settled on the couch beside her.

'I wish to thank you for coming to help our family and invite you to stay with us for as long as you like. Your luggage has already been taken to the palace, and my son will bring you there when he finishes his business.'

Oh, dear—what now?

'That's very kind but I don't know that I can stay,' Sarah began, while her mind searched wildly for an excuse. She was too superstitious to say one of her family was ill in case it came true and she brought illness on someone she loved, but—

'Rahman, or Harry, as I suppose you call him, would

be disappointed if you didn't stay,' Hera told her. 'He is looking forward to showing you his country and introducing you to his family—and Rajah, of course.'

Not wanting to argue that her hanging around was probably the last thing Harry wanted, Sarah seized on Rajah.

And smiled!

'Yes, I'd like to meet Rajah. Harry talked so much about him, but—'

'But there is something between you and my son that would make things awkward?'

Sarah could only stare at the woman by her side. How could she know if Harry hadn't told her?

The she felt the softness of the woman's hand on hers.

'Harry is seeing to things now. We women—and women all over the world—make plans for our children, but the children don't always follow those plans. We know this even as we make our plans, and know not to be disappointed when they don't work out, because all we want is for our children to be happy.'

'But the plans you had—they're important for both family and political reasons, aren't they? Harry loves his country, I can hear it in his voice whenever he speaks of it. He's not a man to walk away from his responsibilities!'

Now Hera smiled, her grey eyes twinkling.

'We knew he was going to be different from the beginning. It wasn't only his passion for an elephant but his insistence on choosing "Harry" for his school name, and his determination to make it to the top of his chosen profession. After the encephalitis, he came back to us a broken man, but now he's back, and whatever path he's chosen will probably be tough because he's not a man who does things the easy way.'

She paused but Sarah knew there was more coming.

'But whatever he does his family will always be behind him. Always!'

She repeated the last word very firmly, although Sarah was still trying to fathom the entire conversation, not just the final declaration.

Uncertain how it had happened, Sarah found herself accompanying the gentle Hera back to the palace in another long, dark limousine. Hera pointed out the city sights, but the city fell behind them as they drove out along a wide, flat road that ran along the shoreline, sunlight dancing off the slightly ruffled blue water.

'I will leave it to Harry to show you around,' Hera said. 'But for now you must rest. The flight, the operation… We have been taking advantage of your good nature. And if you need to contact your family to let them know you will be a little late, there is a private phone in your room.'

If she was dazed by being practically kidnapped by this woman, Sarah was even more dazed—or perhaps dazzled was a better word—by the sight that met her eyes as she entered the palace.

The floor of white marble, veined with fine threads of gold and stretching, it seemed, forever, was littered with bright rugs. Having left her shoes with others outside the door, Sarah found the rugs so soft beneath her feet it felt like walking on a cloud.

An arched opening on the left led into a room even more spacious than the entrance hall. Within, a crowd of women in dazzling dresses ceased their chatter when they saw Hera, rushing towards her like a flock of bright budgerigars.

'The baby is all right?'

'The doctor came?'

'Rahman saved the child?'

The questions flew through the air and, understanding them, and the accents, Sarah realised that all the women must have been educated in England or America.

Although maybe they spoke French and Spanish and even Russian with equal ease.

This was a country that would be full of surprises, and now she wanted so much to stay, to talk to the women, listen to the things they talked about, learn just a little about their culture and customs and how they lived in a world that was being fast-tracked into the twenty-first century.

But staying would mean seeing more of Harry, staying would mean seeing Harry knowing what they'd had was over—unable to touch him, to lean into him, to share his bed...

Unless?

What had Hera meant when she'd said that Harry was seeing to things?

And would Hera have asked her to stay—insist she stay—and that Harry show her around if her presence would be an offence to a bride-to-be?

But being here, being with Harry and not able to touch him, kiss him, sleep with him would be torture.

These frantic thoughts were tumbling through Sarah's head as Hera was hushing the women, telling them she would speak with them soon, and summoning a slight young woman to show Sarah to her room.

'You must rest,' Hera said to Sarah. 'Your luggage is already in the room, and there is a bell to ring for anything you want. Anything at all!'

And Sarah believed her, for hadn't a six-year-old been given an elephant?

Not that she wanted any exotic creature—only Harry.

Although here, wasn't *he* an exotic creature—so far out of her realm she'd barely known him?

Although her body had.

'This way,' a soft voice said, and Sarah sensed she'd said it earlier, while thoughts of elephants and Harry had swirled in her head.

She followed the woman along the length of the great entrance hall, passing rooms off to both sides, done in different colours, but all with the bright carpets on the marble floors and silky-looking curtains swathing all the windows.

At the end of the hall they turned down a passage to the right.

'This is for visitors,' the woman said. 'Madam Hera says you are to go in Yellow—because of your hair she said, although your hair is red, is it not?'

Sarah agreed her hair was indeed red, and as some of the women who had surged around Hera on their arrival had touched her hair and murmured to each other about it, Sarah had realised it made her different.

'Maybe she thought the red hair would clash in another colour of room,' she said, and the woman smiled.

'And maybe, too, it is because Yellow opens to its own courtyard and you can be private.'

Private alone, or private with Harry?

Surely his mother wasn't giving tacit consent to their continuing affair?

Well, hardly affair. And there was no way they could be having sex in a courtyard at the palace no matter how private it might be.

Could they?

No and no and no. It had been a fling and it was over. Harry had duties here, and his position demanded respect, so he could hardly be seen dallying, or even thought to be dallying, with a guest—especially when he was due to marry someone else.

Sarah looked around a room that could have been lifted out of a very posh decorating magazine, and sighed.

It was beautiful, no doubting that. Not *yellow* yellow but more lemon, with some hints of lime thrown in. Pale lemon silk curtains hung across the wide doors that opened onto a covered area outside, with steps leading down to an oasis of green in the small, enclosed garden beyond.

An embroidered silk spread in the same colour as the curtains covered the bed, where pale lime cushions were piled at the end. The lime colour was repeated in the ornate bedside cabinets and the carved-legged writing desk over by the windows that held the phone and heavy writing paper.

Through an arch opposite the windows was what must be a dressing room, walls of cupboards with the same lemon silk on the doors, padded and indented by lime-green buttons.

And through that door a bathroom, the floor and walls the same white marble that provided flooring

throughout the palace, with stacks of pale lemon tow-
els on an antique cabinet, a shelf above it containing
a range of toiletries to shame most department stores.

'You will be comfortable? I will bring tea and you
can rest, Madam Hera says.'

So what Madam Hera says is law, Sarah thought as
the woman left the room. Well, she'd take the tea but she
doubted she would rest. There were too many thoughts
and impressions swirling in her head. Rahman al-Taraq
was there—a little too often—but other things, like
right and wrong, and Harry and fiancées, and family,
and traditions, swirled in the mix until her brain gave
up in sheer exhaustion and she pulled back the coverlet
on the bed, flung the cushions to one side, and slept.

So much for not resting. That was Sarah's first thought
when she woke two hours later. A tea tray sat on the
little writing desk and to her delight the teapot was in-
sulated and the tea still piping hot.

Either that or the almost silent servant had come and
gone at intervals to replace the pot.

However, it had happened, the tea was wonderful,
and the little pastries, hidden beneath a snowy-white
napkin, delicious. So, with something in her stomach,
Sarah debated. Did she want to explore the little courtyard, or shower before she went exploring?

Shower, she decided, but first she had to find her
clothes.

Not difficult when she opened the first cupboard
door and saw her things hanging there, her underwear
neatly stacked in a drawer beside them.

But the clothes brought a sigh. She'd packed for an
English winter and because she'd been in air-condi-

tioned vehicles or the hospital or this coolly luxurious palace, she hadn't felt hot, but she was relatively certain it would be hot outside.

The thought had barely left her when the silent woman returned.

'Madame Hera said there are other clothes you might wish to wear, both European and traditional. You will find them here, and here.'

The woman walked to the other side of the dressing room and threw open more cupboard doors.

It was like walking into an upmarket boutique, as the clothes came in all colours, shapes and sizes and all still held store tags dangling from them—though no sign of price!

Feeling she'd look foolish in a local outfit no matter how the colours called to her after four years of black and white, she chose instead from the first section, sticking to loose linen trousers—black—and a silk shirt.

She'd reached for the white shirt but something seemed to nudge her hand and she lifted out a similar one in emerald green—the colour of the scarf she'd wished for on the island.

'Thank you,' she said, smiling at the woman before collecting her own underwear and heading for the bathroom.

In there, she took a deep breath. She wouldn't take advantage of these people, kind as they were, but would wear the black slacks and some simple shirts while she was here.

And she'd use her own toiletries and cosmetics, no matter how enticing some of the expensive body lotions and face creams might look.

But she did wonder just what happened with this

kind of generosity. She had no idea how many guest rooms the place might hold, but if all rooms were supplied with brand-new toiletries for every guest, there must be awful wastage.

That or the servants must all have perfect skin!

CHAPTER SEVEN

HERA HERSELF CAME to collect Sarah to take her to dinner.

Sarah had just returned from a short sortie into the courtyard and realised that whatever she wore during the day it would have to cover all her skin, as, at dusk, the air was still hot, so by day the sun must be fierce.

Although maybe she'd be gone tomorrow.

Maybe Harry would realise the impossibility of their being here together, and what?

Ask his mother to rescind the invitation?

Hardly.

So he'd avoid her. That would be the best. Hera would ask someone else to show Sarah Ambelia…

'Please don't think we are offering gifts with the clothes we have for visitors to wear,' Hera said, after checking out Sarah's outfit. 'We have the clothes available for those who don't intend a visit here and would have nothing suitable to wear. I think it would be best for you to choose some of our traditional tunics and trousers for daytime, to protect your beautiful skin.'

'But—' Sarah protested, before a small hand on her arm stopped her objection.

'You must not think that anything is wasted. If visitors do not wish to take with them the clothes, or, for that matter, the toiletry items they have used, we pass them on to several houses we have for women from less fortunate circumstances, women who are escaping abusive husbands or families, or who have nowhere else to go.'

Sarah nodded. She knew such organisations existed back at home, and in Australia, even some that took half-used bottles of shampoo and other toiletries.

But here?

Hera must have read her thoughts, for she smiled a little sadly and said, 'Unfortunately it happens everywhere, my dear. People are people all over the world. But, come, we have only a few of the family in to dinner tonight, but they will be anxious to meet you.'

Because of the baby? Or to check out suspicions of a connection between her and Harry—Rahman?

Sarah followed Hera back towards the front of the building, turning off through another arch about halfway down the hall. Although the room was large, it was so full of people she had to wonder just how big the al-Taraq family was if this was just a few of them.

Then Harry was there—Rahman, for he was in his robes—but the hand that touched hers and fired her skin was definitely Harry's.

This was bad, worse than bad—horrendous. How could she be close to him and not look at him, touch him, remember what they'd shared?

'I will not introduce you to all of them at once,' he said, and she realised she should have added listen to him to the list. 'But my other sisters and my brother-in-law and a favourite aunt or two—that will do for tonight. Are you up to it?'

He sounded as if he was flirting.

But they'd never really flirted.

Maybe because she'd forgotten how and their attraction had been strong enough to skip that bit.

But looking up at him, seeing the smile in his eyes, yes, he was definitely flirting.

'And just how many more relations are there that that will do for tonight?'

'Countless,' he said, with a chuckle that stirred every nerve in her body.

Heaven forbid, she was here in a palace, with the man she…loved?

'I don't think I should be meeting any of them,' she muttered at him as the possibility that her feelings might run that deep shocked her into anger.

'It is all right, Sarah,' he assured her. 'Everything will be fine. Just relax and enjoy yourself.'

Relax and enjoy herself in a room full of exotic strangers?

'Just for me?' he murmured, and her bones melted at the smile accompanying the words.

'Why not?' she responded, deciding he was right. Whatever happened in the future, there was no reason not to enjoy the present—and what a stupendous and astounding present it was.

So she allowed herself to indulge in the pleasure of Harry's hand on her elbow, in the warmth of his body close to hers.

He guided her through the crowd and she nodded and smiled and turned away thanks and praise for her coming to help the family, all the time wondering how many of the women were seeing through their 'professional colleagues' act and wondering just how well they knew each other.

Probably all of them because in between introductions Harry was whispering in her ear, teasing her with memories of other whispers.

And she was responding, with quick retorts and, well, almost flirting.

'Time for dinner,' Harry said, giving her elbow a secret little squeeze.

He ushered her towards the back of the room, and Sarah realised it was nothing more than a very large ante-chamber, opening out through more arched doors to a splendid spacious area, a huge mat already loaded with platters of food dominating the middle of it.

'We do have rooms with dining tables and chairs,' Harry said quietly in her ear, 'but tonight with all the women's gossip antennae twitching in the air, the sheer numbers meant we needed to eat in here.'

He led Sarah to one of the long sides of the mat where Hera already sat, her legs tucked neatly to one side. Several other women were sitting now, so Sarah followed their lead, tucking her legs to the side, the cushion beneath her making the position quite comfortable.

She looked around, noticing for the first time that there were children present—a lot of children. They must have been lost in the crowd of adults or maybe had been playing outside.

'The men, like men everywhere, I believe, will gather at the far end,' Hera said, nodding her head to where Harry was striding along the side of the room.

'That way,' Hera added with a sly smile, 'they can pretend to be above the gossip, although they will insist on hearing every word of it from their wives when they get home.'

'You are comfortable to sit like this?' a voice on Sarah's other side asked.

Sarah turned to look at the woman. She was one of Ha—Rahman's sisters, she was sure.

'When I came home from school and university, it would to take me ages to get used to it again, and even now we sit on chairs at a table at home, so my legs aren't as supple as they used to be.'

The woman was beautiful, a red tunic giving her classic features, smooth olive skin and deep brown eyes a radiance that Sarah could only envy.

'What did you study at university?'

Sarah wished she remembered the woman's name but most of her mind had been on not revealing just how much pleasure a simple touch on her elbow could bring.

'I got a First in psychology,' the woman said. 'I thought it might help me fathom just how this family works.'

She smiled and gave a little shrug.

'It hasn't helped,' she added, 'but I'm useful around the hospital both with patients and staff.'

She studied Sarah for a moment before speaking again.

'I suppose you're sick of people thanking you for what you did for Miryam's baby, but we do all appreciate it. You're probably wondering why Rahman didn't ask one of his old colleagues from London, but—'

'But apart from having to see and talk to them, which would have hurt him immeasurably, he wouldn't have wanted to insult them by standing in on the operation, which was obviously what your sister wanted.'

'And *I* did psychology!' Neela—she was Neela,

Sarah remembered—said, smiling again and patting Sarah's hand.

'You must love him very much to have seen all of that,' Neela said, and Sarah was so flummoxed she dropped the piece of bread she was eating and stared at the other woman—probably with her mouth agape.

'Me?' she finally managed. 'Harry? Love? No, no, you have it wrong—we're colleagues, maybe friends, although we've not known each other long, that's all.'

The words must have come out in such a mangled mess that Neela patted Sarah's hand again, while Hera, on the other side, nodded as if with satisfaction.

The meal was superb, platter after platter of delicious food, some with tastes Sarah recognised, others new and different.

'You have seen the resort Rahman has built?' Hera asked.

'Yes. It's very beautiful and the research he's funding at the laboratories there is very important.'

'Ah, but is it enough?' Neela asked, and without thinking Sarah shook her head.

She turned her attention to a small ball of nuts and seeds that Hera had put on her plate, but Neela was persistent.

'And?' she asked.

Sarah shrugged, still hoping to avoid the discussion.

'I know him well,' Neela said, 'and love him so I— all of us—only want the best for him.'

Sarah turned to look at the woman who was still probing—a psychologist's probing or a sister's?

'When we first met,' she admitted to Neela, 'I accused him of opting out of the paediatric surgery he was so good at—of walking away when he still had so much to offer current and future surgeons, even if he couldn't operate.'

She paused but something in Neela's eyes forced her to continue.

'I think I hurt him quite badly,' she admitted.

'Did he hit back at you?'

Sarah stared at the other woman in disbelief.

'It's not witchcraft or even psychology, but I know my brother well. He only hits back when he's cornered and refuses to admit to something he's accused of.'

Sarah just shook her head.

How they'd got onto the topic of her and Harry's meeting at Wildfire—memories of which still had the power to hurt her—she didn't know, but the way Neela spoke of her brother only made Sarah feel more deeply for him and his pain from the loss of the work he'd loved.

'So what are you going to do about getting him off this wild circling of the world, checking this, checking that, and back into the work he loves?'

'Me?'

Sarah was so astonished by the question the word came out as a squeak.

'Yes, you! You're a colleague.'

Something gleamed in Neela's dark eyes. Was it suspicion they might be more than that, or was she simply attempting to sort out her brother's life?

'Yes, but in a minor way. Not in the same league as your brother—not anywhere near where he was, and even could be.'

'Yet you've had him back in Theatre, a place he'd sworn he'd never see again, not once but twice.'

Sarah breathed deeply. She was drowning here, drowning in Neela's persistence.

Yet still she had to protect the man she…

Loved?

Surely not—not in four or five days. Love didn't happen that way.

'Well?'

Had her face changed? Had Neela read something in it as the shock of the random thought hit her?

She could handle this!

'They were both emergencies,' Sarah said firmly. 'Now, tell me, I don't think Harry ever said where he was kept, but is Rajah here at the palace?'

'Nice change of topic,' Neela told her, but she was smiling as she spoke so Sarah guessed she wasn't offended.

'You haven't met Rajah yet?'

It was Sarah's turn to smile.

'I arrived, went to the hospital, played Harry's hands for the operation, then came here, slept, showered and here I am.'

'I suppose it has been a big day for you, but I'll tell Rahman you were asking. He'll probably introduce you to Rajah tonight. It's not far to walk.'

Neela was smiling again but although Sarah couldn't read guile in the lovely eyes, she guessed it was there.

But why?

She had to have missed something somewhere. Harry—Rahman—was supposed to be marrying some woman chosen by his family, so why was his sister suggesting the pair of them have a walk after dinner, probably in moonlight?

Please, let there not be moonlight…

Sarah looked along the rows of people seated comfortably at the sides of the mat, and in spite of his traditional clothes picked out Harry easily.

Because he was looking at her?

You *will* not blush, she told herself, although she could already feel the heat crawling up her neck.

She coughed to cover her confusion then remembered Harry moving close to her, patting her back, turning it into something else—a first embrace.

She glanced his way again but he was speaking to a man in a business suit by his side.

'That's my husband he's talking to,' the super observant Neela told her. 'Most of the menfolk aren't here tonight. My father and Miryam's husband will be at the hospital until they are sure the baby is out of danger, while my other brother is overseas at present—America, I think, maybe at the United Nations—and the husbands of the other women avoid what they call "gossip gatherings".'

Neela paused then added, 'But that doesn't stop them giving their wives the third degree when they get home. I think men are probably worse gossips than women, although they'd never admit it. Do you agree?'

'I've not really thought about it,' Sarah answered honestly, not having had many men close to her in recent years to judge such a thing.

Although…

'My husband hated gossip,' she said. 'Working in a hospital, which are always hotbeds of it, he used to talk about how even the smallest of stories doing the rounds could grow into something large enough to break up a marriage, or hurt someone badly in some other way.'

'Your husband?'

Of course Neela had seized on that!

'He died,' Sarah said, and turned her attention to Hera before Neela could probe further.

'This pastry is delicious,' she said to the older woman. 'Is it a traditional recipe?'

Hera smiled at her.

'Neela wearing you down, is she? I'd like to say it's because of her job, but she's always been the most inquisitive of all my children and definitely closest to Rahman.'

'She's been very kind,' Sarah said weakly, suddenly aware that Hera would have heard most, if not all, of the conversation.

But Hera must have understood because she talked about the pastry, soaked with lemon and honey, and other traditional dishes; about the bread that was made fresh every day, and how oil and dates had been stored in the nomadic days of the family.

Sarah listened, mesmerised by the stories of the past that Hera told, Neela joining in from time to time, prompting her mother's memory or offering her own favourite stories.

'I'm glad to have a settled life,' Neela said, 'but the desert stays in the soul of our people. All of us have to get out beyond the palace walls to listen to the silence or the wind shushing the sand against the dunes, to feel the sun warm us through to our very souls. I think maybe Rahman forgot that in his frenetic journeys around the world.'

Hera nodded then smiled as she added, 'But he is home now, and for that we must be thankful.'

'That and other things, I suspect,' Neela said, but

Hera ignored her, instead directing Sarah's attention to a new platter of desserts that had arrived in front of them.

She tasted coconut in the dessert and again looked along the mat...

He couldn't help but glance her way, checking her as she sat demurely there beside his mother.

It was an unbelievable sight in some ways, but there she was—visible as well as present in the air around him, for he could feel her presence, too.

Sarah...

Neela's husband was telling him about some great business deal he'd pulled off, but Rahman—he *was* Rahman here, although to Sarah he was Harry—well, whoever he was, wasn't quite as fascinated in the story as his companion thought him.

He was too caught up in wanting Sarah—Sarah, who'd entered the ante-chamber with his mother, a vivid green shirt framing her pale face and flaming hair.

Having only seen her in black and white, the sight of her had somehow filled his heart with gladness that she was here, in his home, except...

He wanted her, wanted her more badly than he'd ever wanted anything, even the continuation of his career, but of course he couldn't have her, not physically, not here in Ambelia, where jungle drums were as nothing compared to the whispers of the sands.

So the want ached inside him as he nodded to keep his brother-in-law convinced he was rapt in the story, and ate, and tried not to look along to where Sarah sat.

Neela was beside her—that was dangerous. Neela could draw out secrets from a stone.

Beautiful, that's how she looked—Sarah, not Neela.

'Are you actually interested in what I'm telling you?' his brother-in-law demanded, and Harry smiled and shook his head.

'Not really. I must be tired—the flight home, the baby…'

Stupid excuses really when all of the family were almost as at home in their jets as they were on the ground, and the baby's situation had never been drastic.

'Worried about the changes to your future? Neela tells me the woman's changed her mind.'

Harry shook his head at the speed with which news travelled in this country. He and his mother had only spoken to Yasmina's mother that afternoon.

Now, *that* had been fun!

He'd felt such a worm, but even if nothing eventuated between himself and Sarah, he'd known he couldn't, in all fairness, marry another woman.

Meeting Sarah again, maybe even loving her—could it be love? He had no idea—but even if it wasn't love—

'I cannot believe this!' he muttered to himself.

'That the woman broke it off? You didn't even know her. It shouldn't bother you,' his brother-in-law protested.

Harry—he was Harry when he was thinking of Sarah—shut his lips tightly so the growl that had threatened to escape was captured unspoken.

But not unfelt—

Was this what frustration felt like?

He'd been shocked and angry when he'd learned he couldn't operate again, but he'd slapped away the useless emotions and plunged into other work.

Probably so he didn't keep thinking of the loss.

But he hadn't been frustrated.

Only too aware the word was more used in a sexual context than a general life kind of frustration, he was now feeling both.

Frustrated that he couldn't touch the woman he— well, wanted to touch, and frustrated that his life no longer provided a clear path in front of him.

When he'd taken up the search for an encephalitis vaccine he'd been drawn into other activities that had kept him constantly busy, but now?

Was it because the vaccine, for some forms of the disease, was about to go to clinical trials that he was no longer satisfied, or had Sarah's dig about minions being able to do what he did, dug deeper than he'd realised?

Then, being back in Theatre again, not once but twice...

This time the growl did escape but fortunately his brother-in-law was telling his neighbour on the other side about his latest business coup so it probably went unnoticed.

He glanced towards Sarah again and saw his mother rising from her place, Sarah and Neela with her. As the senior male present, it was his *duty* to escort his mother from the room, wasn't it?

He rose lithely to his feet and moved quickly towards them, taking his mother's arm to lead her to one of the sitting rooms where coffee would be served.

Behind him, people were standing, jostling each other, talking in louder voices now the feast was over, but he only had eyes for Sarah, and ears for the murmur of her voice as she asked Neela what happened next.

'Next I think Rahman takes you to meet Rajah,' his irrepressible sister said, throwing him a wink over their mother's head.

'What a good idea,' his mother said, and Harry frowned.

It would be just like his sister to have sussed out that there was something between them, but for his mother to be pushing them together?

'Go with Rahman,' his mother said, detaching her arm from his hand and easing Sarah towards him. 'I will explain to the family that you are tired but need some fresh air before you retire.'

After which, for his benefit, he knew, his mother repeated, 'Fresh air.'

Neela grinned at him, but Sarah was looking so lost he took her elbow and drew her away from the head of what had become a procession towards the room where coffee would be served.

'You look beautiful,' he told the woman beside him, as he led her down the long hall towards the rear of the main palace building.

'Well, I'm not sure about that, but I can tell you I've never been so nervous in my life. I had no idea what was going on in there.'

'Neela pressuring you for answers?'

Sarah looked at him now, and smiled.

'Just a bit!' she admitted. 'But I doubt she got much she didn't know. She's aware you're unhappy away from the job you love. I think your mother knows that, too.'

Harry shook his head.

'Perceptive women in my family,' he muttered. 'Did they, perhaps, come up with answers to my plight? They know full well I can't operate any more.'

'But you could still be involved,' Sarah insisted, stopping to look directly at him as she spoke.

He shrugged his shoulders, and nodded to the man

who was opening the wide back door for the pair of them, and producing, to Sarah's obvious surprise, the shoes she had kicked off at the front door what seemed like another life ago.

'I think that's where we came in,' he said. She heard what could only be a rueful note in his voice.

'That was only my opinion,' Sarah protested, 'and you'd awoken bad memories, so I struck out at you, but that doesn't mean what I said was wrong.'

'Heaven save me from opinionated women,' Harry grumbled, but the woman by his side didn't respond. Instead she stood and gazed around her, apparently taking in the beauty of this, the kitchen garden, with its neat rows of citrus and stone fruit trees, a fountain playing in the centre of the path that lay between the rows.

'It's an orchard but you've made it beautiful with symmetry and patterns like the carpets inside,' she murmured.

It was Rahman who appreciated the compliment but Harry who took pride in the woman who had seen the design for what it was.

'We try to echo the patterns of carpets in all our gardens,' he said, taking her hand and bringing it to his lips to kiss it lightly on the back.

He felt her shiver of response, and his own acceleration of the need he'd felt since she'd first arrived in Ambelia.

And cursed...

It was a dream.

Being here with Harry, in this fantasy palace with smooth marble floors and carpet gardens beyond the doors, and on her way to meet an elephant.

She was asleep—it had to be a dream—but the surge of feeling through her body when Harry's lips brushed her hand suggested that she must have been awake.

Awake, and oh, so aware of the man beside her...

But he was who he was—Rahman here, not Harry—so a furtive kiss beneath a sculpted apricot tree was not going to be an option.

She could smell the faint hint of roses in the water in the fountain—more fantasy, a land where fountains sprayed rosewater—and walked towards it by the side of the man she couldn't kiss.

And she knew with terrible certainty that she shouldn't have come—shouldn't have answered his plea for help, for all he'd answered hers.

For seeing him again, having him beside her like this, she couldn't help but realise the holiday wasn't over—if what they'd had had really been a holiday romance.

Not for her, anyway.

'He's down this way,' Harry said, breaking into her musings and guiding her down a side path where raised beds, set out in precise geometric patterns, held garden vegetables.

Sarah told herself to lighten up, to relax and enjoy the wonder of this new experience—to set aside all other thoughts and feelings and live for the moment.

Easier thought than done when Harry's light touch on her arm joined them, providing a conduit for messages to hum between their bodies.

Although that would probably be happening without the touch, she admitted to herself, then realised they'd left the garden through an arch in a tall earthen wall and were entering what appeared to be a jungle.

'A jungle in the desert?'

Harry laughed.

'With water we can grow anything, even jungles, and while the sea along one of our borders provides us with water for desalination, we will never be without it.'

Another gate, again through high earth walls, this one carefully locked with a key code for entry.

Harry called and to Sarah's delight an animal—probably an elephant—answered. Then, rumbling towards them from the shadowed trees appeared the huge bulk of the animal he called Rajah.

'But he's beautiful,' Sarah whispered, awed by the huge beast who stood so quietly in front of them.

She reached out and touched the rough hide on his trunk as Harry made formal introductions.

'Sarah, Rajah. Rajah, Sarah.'

The big beast seemed to nod, and Sarah stepped back a little, needing to take him in more fully.

'I've never been this close to one before—never realised just how big they are.'

'He's a beauty,' Harry said, so much pride in his voice Sarah had to laugh.

Harry looked at her for a moment, then he, too, laughed.

'Some first date for a woman—being introduced to an elephant.'

Sarah studied his still-smiling face.

'Is it a first date, Harry?' she asked.

'I think so,' he said. 'I know we skipped that bit on the island but, given the circumstances, I thought I could make up for it here. Take you places, show you things, while we get to know each other better.'

'But are you free to do that? Your mother said something about you seeing to things, but are you free?'

He frowned and she wondered, if he'd broken the arrangement, just how hard it must have been for him.

'I could never have married another woman while feeling the way I do about you. I'm not even sure how that is, which is why we need to go back to the beginning, leaving out the lust part and just get to know each other.'

'And why would we want to do that?' Sarah asked, as too many emotions jostled in her head.

He grinned at her.

'Well, for a start the lust part is impossible here, where every move we make will be watched and broadcast far and wide. I do have *some* responsibility to my family. I hadn't thought it through—I needed you for the op, but I also needed to see you, not even considering that *seeing* each other would be all we'd be able to do.'

'And fully clothed at that,' Sarah teased, as she realised just how he must have felt. 'But why the courtship?

The smile disappeared, and he frowned slightly.

'Because it's the right thing to do,' he said firmly.

Whatever, she decided. If it meant spending a little more time with him, even time made agony because they couldn't touch and kiss, she'd take it.

'Okay,' she said, then to her surprise he took her carefully in his arms and kissed her. Not a heated kiss of passion, like ones they'd shared before, more a first-date kiss, a goodnight kiss…

Or was *goodbye* lingering behind it?

CHAPTER EIGHT

SARAH DIDN'T ASK, simply satisfied to be with Harry as they talked beside the elephant then wandered back through the beautiful orchard, hands linked and bodies touching, and back into the palace.

'I think I'll show you the souks—the markets—tomorrow,' Harry announced as he handed her over to another young woman. 'Lea will take you back to your room and bring breakfast in the morning. Is eight too early for you? I would like to get out before it gets too hot.'

It was beyond weird, Sarah decided, listening as Harry spoke to Lea, apparently giving her orders for the morning.

'I have told her to make sure you have something suitable to wear—well covered so the sun doesn't damage your skin.'

Such ordinary words, but his eyes were saying other things.

Saying that he cared about her?

Loved her?

She frowned and he reached out and smoothed the frown away.

'Don't worry, everything is arranged,' he told her. 'And tomorrow I will show you the souks.'

His fingers slid down to rest lightly on her cheek.

'Goodnight, Sarah,' he said, then turned and walked away.

'This way,' Lea said, her English clear, unaccented.

So why had Harry spoken to her in their native tongue? Had he said more than telling her to make sure Sarah covered up?

'He told me to make sure I take special care of you,' Lea said, apparently reading Sarah's mind. 'It is unusual for him to speak our language in front of a guest so you must be very important to him.'

Was she?

He'd said not to worry—everything was sorted—but was he speaking of the marriage arrangement? Was it because it had been sorted—his betrothal broken?— that he could take her out on dates? He'd said he could never marry another woman while he felt the way he did about her, but what way did he feel exactly? And if that feeling ceased, what then?

Sarah shook her head, suddenly exhausted. She sank down on the bed in the beautiful room and shook her head when Lea offered help.

'I'll be fine, thank you. I'll see you in the morning.'

The girl disappeared on silent feet.

Too tired to do anything more than brush her teeth and wash her face, Sarah stripped off her clothes and climbed into bed. She had pyjamas somewhere in her luggage, but again they were for winter in London.

London. She must phone her parents, let them know when she'd be home.

But when *would* she be home?

And what time would it be there now?

Her brain refused to think about it, so she turned over and went to sleep on a mattress that seemed more like a cloud than something solid, and with a faint rose scent lingering in the pillows beneath her head.

Roses and Harry and an elephant called Rajah—they'd be entwined in her mind forever.

That was her first thought on awakening to a bright, sunny day—perhaps all days were bright and sunny here—and Lea bringing in a tea tray, asking what she'd like for breakfast, offering to fix a platter of the things they usually ate.

'That sounds lovely,' Sarah told her, sitting up with the bedclothes wrapped around her.

As soon as Lea left, she leapt from the bed, had a quick shower, and pulled on a clean towelling dressing gown that was folded on a shelf in the bathroom.

Decent now, she poured some tea and took it across to the window so she could look out at the small court-yard garden while she drank it. There was something magical about it because, just looking at the patterns of the hedges and paths and the different greens in the garden, she felt at peace with the world.

Yes, she had a 'date' with Harry, and had no idea what would happen next, so she'd just take life as it came, enjoying the company of the man she was pretty sure she loved, for all the impossibility of it.

For now, just being with him would have to be enough.

Harry had an early breakfast with his mother, enjoying the traditional tastes of the yoghurt with honey, thick date bread and milky coffee.

'Are you happy, my son?' his mother asked, and he could only stare at her, for she rarely asked personal questions. But when she did, she would expect an honest answer.

'Not entirely,' he admitted, 'although having Sarah here, being able to show her a little of our country, that makes me happy.'

'You are from very different worlds,' Hera said, watching him over the rim of the wide cup while she sipped her coffee.

'I know that, little mother,' Harry said. 'Just as I know, and I think you know, that my little brother would be a better ruler.'

'So you could move to her world?'

Harry shook his head. He had no idea where Sarah's world would be. She'd escaped to Australia to get over a tragedy but she was rebuilt now. Would she want to continue to live there? Might not her parents want her nearer as they aged?

London! Could he live in London again without regretting every minute of every day that he had lost?

'I don't think the question of either of our worlds will arise, little mother. I think now Sarah has found herself again, she will realise how much the future has to offer her. I may not be part of it.'

His mother was silent. Which was just as well, because when he said those words, he suddenly realised that since breaking the arrangement with the family of the woman he was supposed to marry, he had not considered whether marriage lay ahead for him and Sarah.

He'd just known he couldn't continue to see her—even for a date—while he was promised to someone else.

But in saying the words—the 'not being part of her

life' bit—he'd felt pain, deep within his body, and he knew he wanted her, perhaps needed her, beside him forever.

Somewhere…

'When you look at all the sandals and shoes outside the different doors, I have to wonder how my shoes always end up outside the door I'm going out of,' Sarah said, turning to Harry with a puzzled frown as she slipped on her shoes.

'There's no mystery,' Harry told her, 'as those of us who live here probably have sandals at every door, so the servants know the strange shoes in the line.'

'And know what door the strange-shoe wearer will be using next?' Sarah teased, and Harry smiled.

His mind might be in turmoil over what lay ahead, but his body was so happy to be with Sarah, even if it was only for one more day, that he probably wouldn't stop smiling.

How asinine!

But she did look beautiful. She was wearing traditional flowing trousers in a pale orange colour and a long-sleeved tunic over them, with embroidery around the hem and cuffs of the sleeves in a darker colour, almost the red of her hair.

On top of it all, she'd slapped on a wide-brimmed orange hat.

'Your mother found this for me,' she said, pointing to the hat. 'She's worried I might get burnt but I've used plenty of sunscreen, and you said we'd be back home before the day got too hot.'

Home?

Could Sarah ever think of Ambelia as home?

It was important because he'd realised on this visit that no matter where he lived, Ambelia would always be home.

Just happy to be with Harry again, on their own, out on a date, Sarah sat in the big four-wheel drive vehicle and looked out at the country they were driving through as they left the palace.

It wasn't desert, but rocky, red-gold country, and red cliffs scoured by the wind.

'They're like the cliffs at Sunset Beach, aren't they?'

Harry smiled.

'I thought you'd like them.'

Like I like you, Sarah thought, as her eyes remained focussed on the countryside while her mind mused over 'like' and 'love'—two small words, but very important in the whole scheme of things.

Because they led to bonds, and, no matter how much people thought they could manage on their own, most needed friends and family, people they liked and loved.

And 'hated', probably, but that was a far uglier four-letter word—

'This road ahead is my father's pride and joy.'

Harry's voice brought her out of the internal debate she was having, and she looked ahead to see a wide motorway, lined by palm trees and with a median strip planted with smaller, squatter trees that still looked like palms.

'Dwarf date palms,' Harry said, pointing to the smaller trees. 'My father likes to play around with plants and helped develop those. He says they make it easier for children to eat dates straight from the tree, and every child should have such pleasure.'

The pride in Harry's voice told her how close his family were, something she'd suspected when she'd met so many of them the previous evening.

'That's a lovely idea, but how many of them are skittled by the cars roaring down this motorway?'

'Not one,' Harry replied, pointing an overhead walkway, looking more like an exotic sculpture, with steps twisting down to the median strip.

'Those walkways are scattered along the road—about every two hundred metres—and are built to resemble climbing frames in playgrounds so the kids can have an adventure on their way to grab some dates.'

Sarah was about to ask if they were used when she heard the excited shouts of children racing each other down the twisting stairway.

Children!

There'd been children at the dinner, so obviously they were important to the families.

Don't think about it, just enjoy them.

'Where do they come from?' she asked, seeing the little forms darting among the small trees.

'Beyond the noise barriers are quite large housing developments. A lot of the overseas workers live out this way. Many come from very poor and crowded cities and having space is paradise to them. As the city has grown we have needed them for the skills they bring, from architects and doctors down to people who can drive a back hoe.'

Looking beyond the taller palms, Sarah could now see the noise barriers, painted with various scenes of both desert and the sea.

'And here's the city,' Harry announced, and there it was, tall towers rising from the barren ground into the bluest of blue skies. 'We skirt around it to the old town. There are shopping malls and other stores in the city, but for a taste of Ambelia as it was, we keep the old city mostly undeveloped.'

Ahead, earthen walls like she'd seen at the palace came into view. Harry pulled into the shade by a wide arched gate.

'You can take vehicles inside, but do so at your own risk. The roads are jammed with old cars, bikes, donkeys and camels, but, come, you'll see for yourself.'

They walked through the gate into a world of noise and colour.

'Here on the right are the camel markets. Once a week, breeders bring their camels here to sell or trade. Many people still live in the old way and use camels for transport, but today they are mainly bred for tourism and for racing, and as tourists like pretty camels, there's great competition to breed the prettiest.'

Sarah smiled.

'A camel beauty contest,' she said, looking around the covered stalls where a few of the animals rested.

Harry took her hand and squeezed her fingers— first-date style—and although she tried to tell herself it didn't mean anything, her heart leapt at the touch.

'Now we're into the markets proper,' he said. 'This area is for fabrics and clothes.'

'Yes, well, I could have guessed that one! But how could anyone choose?'

Sarah looked around in disbelief as traditional outfits danced on hangers on both sides of the narrow alley. Bolts of brightly coloured cloth stood amongst the outfits, and trimmings dangled temptingly from rods across each stall.

'No prize for guessing this one,' Harry said, when suddenly they were surrounded by metalware. Large jugs and huge pots, silver, bronze and brass, gleamed in the sunlight, the intricate patterns incised into them flashing out 'buy me' lures.

'The shapes are so beautiful,' Sarah murmured, lifting up a tall, graceful jug, running her fingers down its exquisite lines, thinking of the jug in Harry's bure that had brought them both together.

'They are traditional shapes, going back thousands of years,' Harry told her, as she thought of her luggage and reluctantly put the jug down. 'All such household items, even plates and platters, were made in metal so they could be easily transported without fear of them being broken.'

Sarah moved behind him through the crowds, as aware of him, in this crowded alleyway, as if they'd been alone together. Wanting to touch him, brush lightly at his shoulder, his hand...

'Now the gold. Prepare to be dazzled.'

Harry led her to the right, and she *was* dazzled. Jewellery of every type hung from hooks and rods and stands like trees, right out in front of their eyes in places, so to get down the alley at times they had to walk sideways.

Delicate filigree earrings hung beside chunky gold chains, trailing gold necklaces, up to eight strands in each one, competed with gold bangles and bracelets.

'Who buys it all?' Sarah asked, stunned by such an array of wealth.

'Families,' Harry explained. 'Or lovers, I suppose.'

He grinned at her, then explained.

'It is mainly families. If their daughter takes gold into

a marriage, it is hers forever, so if the marriage breaks down, or her husband dies, she will still have money to live on. These days it is not so important because a husband has to support his wife even if they part, and his family would support his widow. But going back, when people lived in tribes, to avoid too much intermarriage a woman would often be married to a man from far away. The gold meant she would always be able to make her way back home if the marriage didn't work out.'

'I think that's lovely in theory,' Sarah told him, hefting a heavy chain in one hand. 'But would her husband let her go?'

'Usually, yes,' Harry replied, 'although there have been, and always will be, bad husbands and probably bad wives.'

Sarah nodded. It was only too true and confirmed what Hera had said about the necessity for women's shelters.

'So, may I buy you something?'

The question startled her and she looked at the man she was with—then shook her head.

'Not on a first date—or even a second date if we count meeting Rajah as the first.'

Harry smiled at her, and her insides melted.

This was *not* a good idea.

She should have left, flown home that morning. Her and Harry's lives were already complicated enough, and being here, especially in the souk, was a reminder of just how different their worlds were.

But the tour continued, through fresh fruit and vegetable markets, then the smell of fresh baked bread drew them down another alleyway.

'We will stop for coffee and a cake here, if you would

like,' Harry suggested, leading the way into the dim interior of one of many small shops and cafés.

The man at the door bowed his head briefly in Harry's direction, and Sarah realised it had been going on throughout their ramble along the alleyways, people nodding deferentially to the man she was with.

She'd taken the first nods as those of passing acquaintances, but unless he knew everyone in Ambelia the nods must be acknowledgement of his royal position.

Had he nodded back?

Sarah couldn't remember, but thinking of it now as the nodding café owner showed them to a table, she realised just how different this world was.

Not only the wealth displayed at the palace, the wardrobes full of clothes for guests who might never wear them, but the acceptance of and acknowledgement by the people that this man was someone special.

And there she'd been, wandering along behind him, because to her he was just Harry.

Well, not *just* Harry!

'If you've fallen asleep on your feet it's definitely time for coffee, but, I warn you, our coffee is thick and dark and sweet and comes in tiny cups with water to drink with it.'

He took her elbow and guided her to a seat.

Sarah watched him as he sat down opposite her and spoke quietly to the man who was serving them.

But all her attention was on Harry, although in his robes he had to be Rahman, and Rahman *was* a prince. Not only that but he was, for all his dislike of the idea, heir to the throne.

Expected to produce more heirs, to keep the family dynasty going...

The tiny coffee cups arrived with a platter of small buns and cakes and a jug in the shape of the one Sarah had admired in the market, condensation from the cold water inside beading on the intricately engraved design.

She traced the line again with her fingers, picking up a little moisture, thinking about Harry and Rahman and families and history and tradition...

And although she hadn't given it much thought, the robes definitely defined him as regal, as did his bearing and the sense of authority that hung like the robes around him.

He was slipping away from her—from being Harry—or maybe distancing himself from her, hence the platonic 'dates' they were enjoying.

And she *was* enjoying this exploration of a country so different from her own, so she decided the only sensible thing was to keep enjoying it and work out the rest later.

After the coffee and cakes, they went back to the palace, Harry having promised his mother not to keep Sarah out in the midday heat. He touched her cheek as he left her at the door to her room.

'I have some things to discuss with my father, but you have a rest, and at four I will collect you to take you to see *my* sunset!'

His fingers lingered on her skin, caressing it gently, and she longed to put her hand on his, to hold it where it was.

Because right then he was definitely Harry, although the man she'd known was already slipping away from her, leaving Rahman in his place.

* * *

'Later' came much sooner than Sarah had expected. She *had* slept, her body clock adjusting itself, no doubt, and was woken by Lea bringing tea and offering delicacies in case Sarah was hungry.

But sleep had left her head muzzy, too muzzy to think about anything that might lie ahead—too muzzy to think, really.

She showered and allowed Lea to choose her outfit—blue loose trousers with a gauzy blue and green top, embroidered around the neck with green thread and sequins.

'Surely that's too fancy for a drive to the desert?' Sarah protested, but Lea insisted it was perfect.

When Sarah was dressed, Lea handed her a scarf, draping it around Sarah's face.

'I don't think so,' Sarah said. 'I don't want to pretend to be someone I'm not. The tunics and trousers are common sense, but unless it is a special day and I need to keep my hair completely covered, I think I'll take the hat.'

'But it's orange,' Lea protested. 'And the scarf is big enough to wrap around your shoulders if it becomes cool.'

Sarah took both, but the hat, when she put it on, did look terrible with the outfit, so she slathered on extra sunscreen and hoped the setting sun would be gentle on her skin.

Harry was waiting by the door in the big entry hall, and he was Harry again, dressed in pale cream chinos and a dark grey shirt. Her heart did that silly flip it insisted on doing when she first caught sight of him, and she realised that, instead of sleeping, she should have been doing some serious thinking.

Too late now, her body told her, reacting with delight to his touch on her elbow.

She was ravishing, Harry decided, as Sarah, escorted by Lea, seemed to glide towards him.

From her long, slim feet to the tip of her vibrant red hair, she was just gorgeous! The colour of the tunic brought out the green of her eyes, and made her skin seem even paler in contrast.

He wanted to touch her, to hold her, to whisper some of what was in his heart, but good manners and protocol dictated he simply take her hand and raise it to his lips.

Colour crept into her face, and a flash of something lit her eyes. Excitement? Happiness?

'You look beautiful,' he said, and she smiled.

'Thank Lea for it—she tells me what to wear.'

She turned to Lea, but the girl had already disappeared on soundless feet.

'It is not the clothes that make you beautiful but the woman inside them,' he said, hoping he was making sense because for some reason he felt like a schoolboy—a youngster on his real first date. 'Come,' he said, steadying her while she put on her shoes. 'Today you're going to see my sand.'

That was better. He was back in control.

'And feel it run like silk through my fingers?' she asked, and he smiled, remembering the conversation on the beach.

His body tightened as he remembered the aftermath of that conversation and the aftermath of most conversations on the beach. He wanted her so badly, but having spoken to his father about his brother succeeding to the throne instead of him, and receiving his father's blessings for a marriage to this woman, he now had to be extra-careful how he was with her, for he didn't want the faintest hint of gossip to sully her name.

Bearing in mind, of course, that she might not want him.

That thought disturbed him so much he shut the door of the car more forcibly than he should have, winning raised eyebrows from the beautiful woman who was causing him so much gut-wrenching stress.

He reached out and touched her thigh, his hand low where no prying eyes would see the gesture.

'I want you so badly it's driving me insane,' he muttered, then he removed his hand, placed it on the steering wheel and drove sedately out of the palace grounds, raising his hand in salute to the gatemen who stood as the vehicle approached.

'Are they guards?' Sarah asked, and, glad to have his mind diverted, he explained.

'We do have some security but it's largely electronic today. Specialists sit in a room surrounded by monitors to keep an eye on things, but the gatemen have been here always, the jobs passing down through generations. I think originally they acted as watchmen in the nomad camps. They are family, too, you know, and these days their sons and daughters go to university, yet there always seem to be some gatemen around.'

'And do they live here?'

Was she asking out of interest, or to keep the conversation going?

To take *her* mind off things she might like to do to him?

He doubted it, although the more time he spent with Sarah the less he felt he knew her, yet a certainty that she was his remained.

He was explaining that all the servants had apartments within the walls when he realised he'd lost her attention.

'Ahh!'

The long, soft sigh came as he turned off the motorway and almost immediately the land on either side of the road gave way from palm trees to red desert sand.

'It *is* beautiful,' she whispered, gazing around at distant dunes and the smaller baby dunes shifting towards the road.

'Do they shift all the time?' she asked.

'All the time,' he agreed, 'but unlike the sea the tide of sand is always coming in. Those little dunes will blow across the road unless they're blown back by machines. We don't like to interfere with nature if we don't have to, but in time the sand would cover every road if left to its own devices.'

He turned into the desert now, along a track that was barely there, driving through a dry wadi then up along the wall of a tall dune. From the top, he knew, they'd have a perfect view of the sunset, and to watch the sunset there with Sarah had suddenly become extremely important.

CHAPTER NINE

THE RED-GOLD DUNES rose and fell as far as Sarah could see, although on the western horizon there were mountains, purple in the distance.

Harry stopped the big four-wheel drive at the top of one of the tallest dunes, and sighed with what sounded like total satisfaction that he was back in his land of sand.

'Sit there for a moment,' he said, turning to her and touching her lightly on the hand.

And while Sarah battled her reactions to a simple hand touch, Harry got out of the vehicle and opened the rear, obviously unloading things.

Whatever he was doing was around his side of the car, but as a flock of birds flew towards the sunset, leaving black shadows on the sand, she looked around more carefully, because this seemingly empty place obviously had life within it.

Here and there little tufts of what looked like the salt-bush that grew in outback Queensland could be seen, some so nearly covered with sand that only a few leaves showed.

And leading away from those leaves, the footprints of a small animal.

Harry blocked her view. He was at the door, opening it, putting out his hand to steady her as she climbed out.

And he kept her hand in his as he led her to where he'd unrolled a carpet and thrown large cushions down on it. A small fire had been lit just off the edge, while on it sat a silver tray with two matching glasses and two tall jugs. Little dishes of nuts and dates surrounded the jugs and a single red rose lay beside them.

Sarah's heart flipped at the rose then she reminded herself that in this country red roses probably didn't mean *I love you*. In fact, they probably had no significance at all…

'You've made us a picnic,' she said, delighted by the scene, whatever the red rose meant.

He led her to the carpet, and she sank down on it, tucking her legs sideways, as she'd learned to do.

He sat between her and the tray, shifting it so they could both reach the offerings.

'I've water or my mother's special juice,' he said. 'Or there's coffee in the car if you'd prefer that.'

'Definitely the juice,' Sarah told him, watching hands that had fondled her body lift the jug and pour juice for her.

'Cheers,' she said, lifting her glass to his, mainly to break the tension that, for some reason, was coiling inside her.

You're here to see the sunset, she reminded herself. Nothing more.

She sipped her drink, Harry lounging now beside her, the sun dropping swiftly and the colours of the sand reflecting back the sky of brilliant orange, red, and yellow.

'It's beautiful,' she murmured, as the full extent of this special sight struck her. 'So beautiful!'

'But wait,' Harry said, touching her lightly on her thigh and starting all the physical reactions again. 'Wait until it sinks and the softer colours come.'

And come they did, the pinks and mauves, and blues and purples, making the desert seem more like the sea than a vast stretch of sand.

'It's like the colours of the water over the reef.'

Harry smiled.

'That's exactly what I thought the first time I flew into Wildfire, only the other way around, of course. That the colours of the water over the reef was like my desert sands at sunset.'

He eased himself to a sitting position and took her hand.

'Do you like my sunset, Sarah?"

He sounded so serious, as if this was very important to him, that Sarah could only nod.

He moved closer, put his arm around her shoulders.

'I know it's a strange question for a third date,' he said, his voice so deep and husky it reverberated in her bones. 'But will you marry me?'

The shock struck Sarah like a lightning bolt, solidifying all her body as if she'd turned to stone beside him.

She stared towards the fire, now more visible in the gathering dusk.

Harry had asked her to marry him.

Marry Harry?

As her body began to return to flesh and blood and nerves and even tingling excitement, she knew she had to tread very carefully.

To think before she spoke…

But who could think through such a startling question?

So don't answer—well, not right away.

'Did you bring me out here to ask me this?'

She'd shifted slightly away from him and turned to look at him, catching a small, wry smile playing around his lips—lips she'd kissed with such passion that simply seeing them made her feel hot all over.

'I brought you out here to see the sunset,' he said, and she believed him, although his hands were shaking as he lifted the jug to pour more juice. 'The question just seemed to come out, as if it was the natural thing to do.'

Sarah took a deep breath. Somewhere inside her a voice was prompting a 'yes' reply, but she'd had enough trouble working out who she was—and making a new life for herself after the accident—without marrying a man who was as torn and broken, although in a different way, as she had been.

She took his hand and traced the back of it, the veins and bones and tendons, with her fingers, before lifting her head to look directly at him.

'I don't think I can, Harry,' she said quietly. 'It's not that I don't love you—I've been fairly certain about that for some time, but our worlds would clash, we wouldn't fit. Your life, when you're not off doing the encephalitis stuff, should be here, with your family, keeping the traditions going, caring for your people, while me, I have to finish out my contract in Australia, then I think I'll return to England.'

She couldn't tell him why—afraid it would be too painful for him, hurt the man she loved too much.

'To try to get back into paediatric surgery,' he said

quietly, a statement, not a question, as if he could read her dreams.

He put his free hand over hers, trapping it between his, and to Sarah it felt like goodbye.

'Yes, I've dithered long enough,' she said. 'The two operations... They recharged that desire that your talk at GOSH first aroused in me. I want to put the past behind me and move on.' She paused, but knew she had to continue. 'And I need to get home—now. I've loved every minute of being in this amazing country, but I need to get home and see my family, talk to people, and then get back to Oz to finish that job before I can start again. I can't say I'm all that confident, but at least I'll know I gave it a go.'

She was prattling but the tension between herself and Harry was so tight she felt it could explode at any moment, with a force that would hurt them both.

'Can you ask someone to arrange a flight?'

Harry sat on a carpet on his favourite sand dune, watching the final flickers of colour from the dying sun, and felt his world collapse around him.

Not that he'd been expecting Sarah to say yes... Well, how could he have been when he hadn't realised he'd intended to ask her?

It had been a daft idea. Their worlds *were* far too far apart, and although he'd told his father earlier that he didn't want the throne, his life was still a mad rush around the world, checking up on things that were happening in both the scientific and the practical measures he'd set up.

He'd be back on Wildfire before long, to check on

the progress of the clinical trials, and in Bangladesh soon after that.

What woman would want a husband who was never there?

And when he was at home, wherever that might be, how could he live with someone who was doing the job that had been taken from him?

The job that had been his passion?

He squeezed the fingers on the hand he held in his, and much as he wanted to argue and protest, he knew that she was right to turn him down.

'I love you,' he said quietly, and knew he should have said it sooner.

Not, he suspected, that it would have made much difference...

The hand in his moved to tighten its grip.

'I love you, too,' she said, her voice so full of sorrow he longed to take her in his arms and hold her close.

Forever?

She'd made it clear that couldn't happen, so he lifted a handful of sand and placed it in her hand, where she let it slip between her fingers.

'Sand like silk,' she said, remembering his description of it, 'but it's like life as well, isn't it? If we're not careful it slips away because we're too afraid to grab it and cling to it and wring whatever satisfaction and joy and pleasure that we can out of it.'

He kissed her then, restraining the passion burning within him for this was a goodbye kiss...

So much for booking a flight for her, Sarah thought as the limo carrying her turned into the private part of the airfield where she'd arrived.

It pulled up at the foot of stairs leading into the same, or a similar, jet to the one in which she'd arrived.

'Welcome, Dr Watson,' one of the cabin crew greeted her as her chauffeur held open the door. 'If you would give me your passport, I'll see to the formalities while you get comfortable inside.'

Another member of the crew beckoned her up the stairs.

But halfway there she turned and looked back, disappointed that all she could see was the airport and the city beyond it.

'You'll see the desert when we take off,' the crew member told her.

But Sarah knew that had been only part of her disappointment.

Not that she'd expected him to be here.

They'd both agreed last night that their goodbyes would be said in private. Not in the desert but, after dinner with the family, when she'd gone to say goodbye to Rajah.

And remembering Rajah she had to blink back tears, telling herself it was certainly the goodbye and not the kiss that had followed it that she would miss.

But she'd miss more than a kiss from Harry. She'd miss his closeness, miss sharing little moments of the day with him, miss his touch, and the feel of his skin beneath her fingers.

She'd miss him with an ache deep inside her but in time she'd find a smile as well—a smile for the happy memories.

Settled in her seat, seatbelt on, the engines whining as the pilot revved them, she reminded herself that pain lessened with time, and the memories became good friends instead of hurting.

She waited until the plane had crossed the desert, giving her one last glimpse of the red-gold sand, then closed her eyes and slept, waking only for a snack as they approached Farnborough, where, according to one of the crew, they were due to land.

He'd also told her that a car would meet her to take her to her family home in Roehampton, only a twenty-minute drive, she imagined, although she'd never been to Farnborough before, even for an air show.

Harry threw himself back into work, travelling first to Africa where his scientists were struggling to balance mosquito eradication with the preservation of the natural ecosystem.

Spraying worked for a season, but the swamps were still there, and the swamps and waterholes were an integral part of the local landscape and home or source of food to the inhabitants of each area.

The vaccine was the answer, and although clinical trials of the Wildfire vaccine were under way, there was doubt it would work here. The disease mutated according to the area, and sometimes success seemed a long way off.

But he persisted, needing work and the frantic dashing around the world to keep his mind off Sarah.

He could tell himself it had been nothing more than a short affair—a holiday romance, as she'd kept insisting—but images of her played in his head and a word here or a sight there reminded him so strongly of her he'd often have to stop what he was doing and breathe deeply for a moment.

The invitation came as a surprise.

It was waiting for him when he returned home for a brief visit before heading to Asia.

Real mail—a letter—white and thick, like an invitation...

But there was always mail waiting for him, and always invitations to speak at this or that convention.

He threw it in the bin, part of his past, then contrarily pulled it out and shoved it in his travel bag.

He might read it on the plane.

Or not!

But although that part of his life was over, it might be interesting to see who the speakers were going to be and whether any of them might have something new to offer.

He thought no more about it as one of the engineers he'd employed to look at draining a flooded rubbish dump in Bangladesh, with a view to reclaiming the land, was on the flight so it was back to business.

He avoided Wildfire for as long as he could, knowing he had competent people there who could carry on the work.

But even thinking about Sarah brought a clear image of her into his head, right in the middle of some theory about reclaimed land—a smiling, teasing image.

Sarah spent the first week home with her parents doing family things like visiting aged aunts and walking through Richmond Park with the dogs, remembering Bugsy on Wildfire who'd loved a walk...

The second week she began tentative enquiries about the possibility of getting an opening on a paediatric surgery team. She was only too aware that most of the people who could offer such training would be friends of Harry's and one word from him might have made her job easier, but she couldn't hurt him more by asking this of him.

He was with her day and night—well, more at night—because it was easier to escape her thoughts during the day.

But at night she dreamed of the time they had shared, of the passionate and gentle lovemaking between them, of their conversations, and shared laughter, and sitting together on Sunset Beach.

She didn't think about the desert sunset, although its magical beauty was burned into her brain.

That memory was too painful…

He phoned one evening. She was just back from a walk and the smell of the roast beef her mother was cooking for dinner hung around the house.

She answered the phone, thinking it would be an old friend calling back, a doctor with whom she'd trained and who was now a GP.

They were making arrangements to get together for a meal, so there was no premonition of it being anything other than an ordinary call.

'Sarah, I need you.'

Harry's voice…

Harry's voice almost pleading…

Her heart was bouncing around in her chest, her lungs had seized, and her stomach cramped painfully.

'A baby?' she managed to croak.

To her surprise she heard a smile—well, half a smile, a little bit of a smile—in his voice as he answered.

'No, more a pillar—that's what I need.'

'A pillar?'

She took the phone from her ear and checked to see she wasn't dreaming.

'One of those things that support other things,' he continued, although she might have missed a bit. 'I need you to support me, be my pillar.'

Long pause.

Was he gone?

No-o-o-o!

The wail came from her heart and then he was back again, his voice in her ear.

'To prop me up.'

She heard a deep intake of breath then his words came out in a rush.

'I've been asked to speak at a symposium in London, at GOSH, and at first I threw the note away, then I picked it out of the bin and tucked it into my luggage, and when I had to go back to Wildfire I looked at it and saw what it was and I heard you in my head telling me it's what I should be doing—working in the field I loved and was good at. So I phoned someone and said yes and now I'm getting nervous. It's next Tuesday and they've booked me into a hotel, the Russell, quite close to GOSH and the British Museum, if my talk gets boring for you, and it's at the opening of the three-day talk-fest and I wondered if you'd come.'

'Yes!' Sarah said, and wondered if he could hear her smile, which was so wide he could probably see it reflected on the moon if he was looking.

'That's it?' he asked—or maybe demanded.

'Yes,' she said again, because that really *was* all there was. The rightness of it all, and seeing him again, and maybe, just maybe, talking him into returning to the work he'd loved and lost.

'I'm coming in on Sunday. I'll phone you with the time. Someone will collect you to meet me at the plane. We'll have a couple of nights together before the show begins. Time to talk…'

Pause…

'Is that all right?'

'More than all right,' Sarah said. 'I'll pack a bag.'

CHAPTER TEN

'THERE'S A VERY large car outside,' Sarah's mother said on Sunday morning, sounding a little put out by the ostentatiousness of a very large car.

'It's how they get around, Mum,' she said. 'But the people are ordinary, friendly, hospitable—just like you and me.'

'Except they live in a palace,' her mother countered, and Sarah realised that although she'd listened to Sarah's tales about Ambelia with interest, she was obviously concerned about Sarah's possible future amidst such wealth.

'Wait till you meet him,' Sarah said, hugging her mother, although the car was waiting. 'He gives his talk on Tuesday evening and we'll come out here on Wednesday, take you and Dad to The Crabtree for lunch and we can sit by the river if it's fine.'

Sarah could see her mother still had doubts, but those, Sarah guessed, were about meeting Rahman al-Taraq, and would be banished when she met Harry.

She said a quick goodbye and went out to the waiting car.

'First to Farnborough to meet the plane,' the driver

told her, and this time Sarah actually noticed what Farnborough airfield looked like.

It was, she realised, like some great futuristic city, only too small to be a city—a village maybe.

It had developed from a small, wartime landing strip to an airfield that catered to the wealthy and privileged, flying in on their private jets for business, a shopping trip, or simply pleasure.

The high-arched dome was more intimidating than welcoming, but Sarah guessed it looked better from the other side.

She waited, moving from one foot to the other in an effort to keep her excitement in check, then, finally, he was there, walking out through sliding doors and just appearing in front of her.

He dropped the small bag he was carrying and drew her into his arms, holding her so close and for so long she wondered if he'd ever let her go.

Not that she wanted to be let go!

Eventually they made their way to the car, joined at shoulder and hip, his arm around her waist.

With the miracle of organisation she was beginning to accept as part of Harry's world, his luggage was already being loaded into the boot, and the driver had the rear door open for them.

Harry spoke quietly to him, then slid in beside her, reclaiming her hand and drawing her close to kiss her again.

'I have never before understood the concept of missing someone,' he said, when he finally raised his head from hers, and brushed his fingers against her cheek. 'But every moment of every day since you left, I have missed you. In my head, and in my heart, and in other parts of my body that we'll leave nameless, you've been a gap and an ache and a sorrow all run together.'

Sarah nodded, her heart too full of happiness for words to form.

'You, too?' he asked, and she smiled and nodded, then kissed the lips that had haunted her dreams for so long.

They spent a very enjoyable hour or so in the car, until the driver announced 'Hotel Russell, sir' and Harry and Sarah broke apart like naughty schoolchildren caught kissing behind the gymnasium.

The driver opened the door on Sarah's side, while uniformed hotel staff appeared from all directions, whisking away Harry's large suitcase and Sarah's much smaller bag on a trolley that would have held five times as much luggage.

Harry took her hand to lead her into the hotel, but Sarah paused, wanting to take it all in. The big old red and cream brick building had large inset windows, and the quiet dignity of a dowager of older times. Inside, it was breathtaking, with marble floors and pillars and a huge chandelier over the central foyer.

'It's not six stars but it's very comfortable,' Harry was saying, 'and close enough to walk to GOSH.'

'I love it already,' Sarah said, although she knew she'd also have loved some cheap flea-pit hotel with Harry for company.

Once registered, they were shown to their suite of rooms, with views out over Russell Square. But views were soon forgotten, because Harry was behind her, holding her close, his desire for her making itself felt.

She turned in his arms, and held him close as she kissed him, remembering how well they fitted together, remembering touches that brought him pleasure, and revelling in the fingers that roamed her body.

'We will *not* hurry this,' he said very firmly. 'I've been waiting so long I refuse to be rushed.'

But somehow that didn't work because, once naked on the bed together, not rushing wasn't an option, the fire between them driving their bodies to take and be taken, to give and be given, to touch, and kiss, and tease, and come together until they both lay exhausted on the bed.

'Maybe next time we'll take it slowly,' Sarah teased, propping herself on pillows so she could look down at Harry's beloved face.

She traced her fingers down his profile, around his lips, and her heart filled with love for this man she'd met by chance, and who had given her back her love of life itself.

She'd slowly put herself back together again, but to find love as deep as this a second time—that was special.

'Thank you,' she said, dropping a kiss on his lips. His eyebrows rose. 'For loving me, for letting me love you.'

For now, that was enough, Sarah decided. The future could take care of itself...

Tuesday dawned bright and sunny, and because Harry had people to see at GOSH, Sarah walked with him to the hospital, a little bit of new excitement fizzing inside her as she'd been accepted on a paediatric surgical team, not here but at Arcadia London Children's Hospital, due to begin in six weeks.

She'd be going back in time to the long and irregular

hours of hospital work, with study on top of that, but it was something she definitely wanted to do.

And something that would occupy all her attention if this little visit with Harry proved to be just that—a small piece of heaven stolen from time.

'Well, are you coming in?' Harry asked as they stood by the statue of Peter Pan and Tinkerbell outside the front door.

'Not until tonight,' she said, then wondered at the look of concern on his face.

'You'll be all right?' he asked anxiously. 'Not too many bad memories?'

She had to smile.

'My memories of that life are all good ones now, Harry. Yes, I wonder about the baby, but all the rest are safely stored away. I've made new memories now and am happy with them, and happy to make more.'

She didn't say 'with you' because beyond tonight she had no idea where Harry's future might lie. She hoped it would be here, but knew it would be a huge step for him to take, to get back into paediatric surgery without being able to operate.

'I should be done by lunch but just in case, let's meet back at the hotel at three—I'll stand you high tea!'

Sarah laughed. Harry was standing her everything on this little holiday and she felt pampered and thoroughly spoiled by his attention.

She kissed his cheek—lip kisses were too hard to break and they were in public—and left, wanting to wander through the museum again, to look at artefacts from the past and think about her future.

It would be with Harry, wherever he was, she'd decided. She could travel with him, learn about his projects, forget the idea of further study...

Couldn't she?

As thinking only confused her, she headed for the Egyptian rooms and peered at mummies preserved for thousands of years, wondering if love had been as hard for people then as it was for her now.

She had lunch in the café beneath the vast, high steel and glass roof, built to provide more space and facilities for the museum, then walked back to the hotel to shower and change before meeting Harry again.

He was late, coming in at four, telling her he'd booked a table for high tea, urging her off the bed, where she'd been reading and dozing, and insisting they go now.

He was fizzing with excitement, and as they stood together in the elevator she could feel it buzzing in his body.

'So tell me what this is all about,' she said, but he smiled and shook his head.

'Soon,' he promised, and because the elevator was empty but for them, he dropped a quick kiss on her lips.

They sat in style at the back of the big open foyer in high-backed armchairs, a table with a snowy white cloth over it in front of their knees.

Sandwiches came first, tiny delicate sandwiches made from different coloured breads with fillings so delicious Sarah ate the lot.

'Now tell,' she said when the waiter brought scones and jam and cream, the scones covered by a pristine white napkin to keep them warm.

He looked at her, grey eyes dancing with excitement, although she thought she could read doubt on his face.

'There's a job,' he said, 'teaching and research. It would give me time to keep an eye on my managers who'll take over the overseas programmes but get me back into what I love.'

He paused, took a scone, and carefully broke it open and buttered it.

'It's the research that interests me most as it involves development of new techniques for operating on babies still in the womb, correcting a lot of congenital problems before the infant is born.'

Sarah's heart lurched, and she reached out and covered his hand with hers.

'It's perfect, something new,' she said, 'something to excite you, and the teaching... That's a bonus for your students because you're the best.'

'Was the best,' he said quietly, and she understood the doubt she thought she'd seen.

'That was then, and this is now,' she said, refusing to let him dampen her excitement. 'And the first breakthrough you make in your research will have you back on the top of the tree again, if that is what you want.'

He didn't answer, studying her instead, thinking...

And now his smile was free of doubt.

'It's not what I want,' he said, confusing her for a moment. 'To be top of the tree again,' he explained.

He reached out and took both her hands in his slightly buttery fingers.

'You're what I want. To live with you, be with you, have children with you if you want them. I want you for my wife, by my side, whatever lies ahead. I learned that when you left, but couldn't see a way forward until now, when we're together again. I know you have your own ambition and I'll be with you all the way, but being offered this position means we can be together, here in London, and it's the being with you that's the most important thing.'

'But Ambelia? Your home? The throne?'

He smiled so gently she thought her heart might break.

'That's all been decided. My brother will make a far better ruler than me, and, deep down, I think my father knows it. Well, the rest of the family does anyway.'

The smile was better this time, but still Sarah held her breath.

'So now I'm yours, if you'll have me? I have my parents' blessing—they both love you already because they have seen how happy you make me. So, my Sarah...'

I will not cry, Sarah told herself, but felt the tears sliding down her cheeks anyway.

The waiter brought little plates of cakes and pastries but she was beyond eating.

'I'll pack them in a box and send them to your room,' he said, when Sarah waved him away. 'Nice for a midnight snack.'

She smiled weakly, then realised they probably would be good at midnight—a midnight feast with the man she loved.

Harry stood on the dais, a lectern before him, dressed as she'd never seen him, in a dark suit, grey shirt and darker grey tie.

He was beautiful, she decided, then wriggled in her seat, for he'd told her the same thing—that she was beautiful—before they'd left the hotel.

They'd returned to their room after the abbreviated high tea, where she'd found an exquisite outfit waiting for her.

'I told the woman in the boutique all about you and she chose it all,' Harry had said proudly, and 'all' it was, right down to filmy underwear and sheer stockings and black high-heeled shoes.

The suit itself was grey, the colour of his shirt, with an emerald-green silk blouse to go beneath it and a small black handbag to finish the outfit.

'Oh, Harry,' she whispered, shaking her head. 'It's lovely, so stylish. I didn't have much reason to wear suits in Cairns.'

He smiled and pulled her close so it was a little while before they both dressed in their finery and made their way to the hospital.

This would be a test for her, Harry thought, holding tightly to Sarah's hand as they made their way through the building to where conferences and symposiums were held.

He was pretty sure it was the first time she'd have been here since the day the accident had taken her husband and child, and it must be taking tremendous courage on her part to be returning.

And she was doing it for him—to be there when he spoke, for the first time in nearly five years, about the work that had been his passion.

'New starts,' she whispered to him as they entered the main lecture theatre, and her fingers returned the squeeze he'd given hers.

'Are you all right?' he asked, and found her smile as reassuring as her words.

'With you beside me, how could I not be?'

He wanted to kiss her, but it was too public a place, and too many old friends and acquaintances were hailing him.

'It may be a crush later,' he said, realising he'd have to speak to these people. 'Do you want to join me?'

'And meet a couple dozen strangers all at once?' Sarah teased. 'No, if you lose me I'll be waiting by Peter and Tinkerbell.'

Expecting nerves, Harry was surprised to find himself at home behind the lectern, talking easily about the history of paediatric surgery, the first operations that now seemed clumsy, even inept compared with work done today.

'But we must move on,' he said, 'to a future where many congenital defects can be repaired in the womb, and investigate ways for problems that can't be handled that way to be done with minimally invasive surgery. Keyhole surgery is commonplace in most theatres now, but less is known about the procedures where that technique can be used on small children, even neonates.'

He paused and felt the attention of every person present in the room, although his eyes found Sarah first.

'For that is the way ahead. That is our holy grail, and here at GOSH, through the generosity of some of our supporters, it will be happening before long.'

He surprised himself as he mentioned a few possibilities, surprised by the fact that part of his brain must have been working on these matters for some time.

Sarah sat and watched him, barely listening to his words. She'd been happy just to be with him, even if only for a few days, but now she could be happy in the present and look forward to even more happiness in the future.

The crowd rose as one, and she realised she'd drifted away from the words he was saying, content just to listen to his voice.

She stood up, clapping with them, clapping because the man she loved had returned to the world he loved.

Sure, there were things they both had to do, but before long they could be together forever.

Forever?

Was she jumping the gun?

No, he'd said forever and she knew he'd meant it. It was just that marriage hadn't been part of the conversation—not since she'd turned him down in Ambelia.

She looked around for him, but he was being mobbed by admirers and well-wishers and she didn't want to deny him that, so she eased out of the room and walked back through the hospital to the little garden where Tinkerbell perched lightly on one of Peter Pan's fingers. Tinkerbell had been added later, she remembered, but the delicacy of the bronze casts always amazed her.

To her, tonight, they were symbols of David and her unborn child, the bronze statues as strong as the memories tucked away inside her head. They would never be forgotten, but it was time to move on, and to move on with joy and anticipation into the life that lay ahead.

That's if Harry did ask her to marry him…

He appeared, as if by magic, and took her hand.

'Will you marry me?' he said.

And this time she said, 'Yes.'

They wandered back to the hotel together, content to be alone.

CHAPTER ELEVEN

GETTING MARRIED, THEY REALISED, was harder than it seemed.

'Dratted people,' Harry muttered, as he shut off his cell phone for the third time that morning.

'Leave it, for the moment,' Sarah told him. 'You're nervous about meeting Mum and Dad, and phoning government offices isn't helping. Besides, Dad will know what to do. He worked in the local council for years, and loves knowing everything that goes on.'

Dad did, and over lunch in the open garden of The Crabtree pub, looking out over the Thames at its most beautiful as it twinkled in rare sunlight, he explained the procedures at the register office.

'You can print the forms off the internet. The first, your request to get married, has to go in twenty-eight days before the date, and another, which lists all the information about yourself, you have to take with you when you deliver the notice.'

He turned his attention to Harry.

'You lived and worked here—do you have residency?'

Harry smiled.

'Scottish grandmother, hence the grey eyes, so I have

dual citizenship, and not only do I have a British passport, I also have a flat in Fulham. It will need a bit of refurbishing as I haven't lived there for a while, although some of the family have used it from time to time.'

'Well, that's the next consideration—proof of residence—a tax notice of some kind.'

The conversation continued, Harry certain he'd be able to provide all the evidence required, but Sarah's evidence would be harder. She knew she had David's death certificate tucked away somewhere but had always refused to look at it.

She felt Harry's hand find hers beneath the table and knew he understood what she was feeling, as did her mother, no doubt, who got on to practicalities.

'With twenty-eight days' notice you might just be able to squeeze it in before you have to go back to Australia and Harry's due in Asia,' she said.

So they discussed dates.

Harry was leaving for Africa the following day but could be back whenever he was needed.

'And if I have a date I can get my parents over,' he said, and Sarah nodded. They'd already decided that the only people they wanted at the wedding were both sets of parents, although Harry had warned her there would be big celebrations to be endured—or enjoyed—when they next returned to Ambelia.

So it was sorted, the wedding date set, Harry seen off to Africa, and Sarah left to wonder just how this had all happened in what seemed like a millisecond of time.

'No time for dreaming,' her mother chided her. 'You might not be doing the full bride thing, but I want you looking beautiful for that man—he deserves it.'

* * *

She was beautiful!

So much so she took his breath away.

Dressed in a deep cream-coloured suit, very simple with a calf-length skirt and fitted jacket, and very pale green shirt underneath it, her red hair swinging free, he just stood and looked, until his mother prodded him and he managed to step forward and take her hand.

They'd had dinner the previous evening, all six of them, so the two sets of parents could meet and talk.

And talk they did, embarrassing both him and Sarah with their reminiscing.

Now they were waiting, waiting to witness the marriage of their children, and he was waiting, too, waiting for a future with this woman he loved beyond all words.

Tomorrow they'd be parting, the jet dropping Sarah at Cairns airport before taking him on to Wildfire. They both had jobs to complete before beginning their London life.

But today and tonight she was his, his to love and be loved by.

'I love you!'

She mouthed the words at him as they went into the very functional room at the register office used for weddings.

He squeezed her hand in response.

A short ceremony, lunch at the five star hotel where his parents were staying, then home to his flat, already refurbished, the renovations overseen by Sarah while he'd made his final mad dash around the world, minions trailing after him to learn the way of things.

Sarah managed to get through the ceremony without crying, enjoyed lunch with their parents at the posh hotel, but as it drew to a close her nervousness increased.

Soon, too soon really, they'd be back at the flat, and she was worried what Harry—or maybe Rahman—would think of it.

The flat, when she'd first seen it, though spacious, had been student style with a bit of minimalist thrown in. Fortunately for her, Hera had come over, and with her mother the three of them had shopped.

Now it was a home, with polished wood floors, soft leather armchairs, a settee with a bright angora throw to wrap around the two of them, and small but functional tables scattered around.

And on the wall and floor were carpets, small and large, colourful, intricately woven pieces Hera had brought over with her.

The dining room was more formal, the glass and chrome table, which Harry had bought at some time, softened by the large silk on silk Persian carpet underneath it, while a long cabinet against one wall held a collection of the beautiful jugs, goblets and platters Sarah had so admired in Ambelia.

And in here the only ornamentation on the walls was a large picture of Wildfire, the cliff ablaze with the colour of the setting sun.

Harry wandered through the rooms, his hand holding tightly to Sarah's, a catch in his breathing the only comment when he saw the living room. But in the dining room, in front of the picture, he took her in his arms and kissed her.

'Beautiful!' he said. 'Both you and my new flat.'

But if he'd liked the beginning of the tour, the bedrooms knocked him off his feet. Three bedrooms, the smallest of which Sarah had refrained from changing much, hoping in the near future it might need balloons and flowers and small animals involved in its decoration. The spare bedroom had the colours of the island, the translucent blue-green waters on the spread, chair and cushions covered with bright reef colours.

'And you're saving the best for last?' Harry asked, as she led him to the main bedroom.

Which she was—well, she hoped it was the best.

She'd used the colours of the desert here, the red-gold of the sand, the paler silk curtains and embroidered quilt, and a soft cream carpet so the colours came alive.

He loved it and apparently he loved her, for the delicate silk quilt was soon thrown aside, and they collapsed together on the bed, holding each other and laughing at the sheer joy of being together—together for now and together always.

They undressed each other slowly—teasingly slow— but Sarah was determined not to crush her wedding finery. This suit would always be special to her, and this time when they returned to the bed it was to make love slowly but passionately, their actions better than words to explain their feelings at that time.

Talk came later, little memories they'd shared, talk of Wildfire and their meeting, of the work that lay ahead— their hopes, their dreams, their futures.

When Harry slid from the bed, Sarah felt his absence but he was back within a minute, kneeling by the bed, opening a box and drawing out the most beautiful necklace she had ever seen.

'This has been given by my family's eldest son to his wife on their wedding day for as long as my people can remember. My mother gave it to me last night.'

He leaned forward and clasped it around her neck, Sarah still wide-eyed in wonder, her fingers going up to touch the brilliant emeralds and small diamonds that glittered between them. The gems were cold against her skin, yet her body burned when Harry added, 'And I doubt they've ever looked more beautiful than they do on you.'

She understood now why he'd insisted on an emerald for her engagement ring, a ring that was now protecting that more precious ring, her wedding band.

She drew him to her, back onto the bed, and they pledged to each other without words but with the jewels between them shining as a bright token of their love.

* * * * *

Don't miss the next story in the fabulous
WILDFIRE ISLAND DOCS *miniseries:*
THE FLING THAT CHANGED EVERYTHING
by Alison Roberts.
Available next month

MILLS & BOON®
Hardback – March 2016

ROMANCE

The Italian's Ruthless Seduction	Miranda Lee
Awakened by Her Desert Captor	Abby Green
A Forbidden Temptation	Anne Mather
A Vow to Secure His Legacy	Annie West
Carrying the King's Pride	Jennifer Hayward
Bound to the Tuscan Billionaire	Susan Stephens
Required to Wear the Tycoon's Ring	Maggie Cox
The Secret That Shocked De Santis	Natalie Anderson
The Greek's Ready-Made Wife	Jennifer Faye
Crown Prince's Chosen Bride	Kandy Shepherd
Billionaire, Boss...Bridegroom?	Kate Hardy
Married for their Miracle Baby	Soraya Lane
The Socialite's Secret	Carol Marinelli
London's Most Eligible Doctor	Annie O'Neil
Saving Maddie's Baby	Marion Lennox
A Sheikh to Capture Her Heart	Meredith Webber
Breaking All Their Rules	Sue MacKay
One Life-Changing Night	Louisa Heaton
The CEO's Unexpected Child	Andrea Laurence
Snowbound with the Boss	Maureen Child

MILLS & BOON®
Large Print – March 2016

ROMANCE

A Christmas Vow of Seduction	Maisey Yates
Brazilian's Nine Months' Notice	Susan Stephens
The Sheikh's Christmas Conquest	Sharon Kendrick
Shackled to the Sheikh	Trish Morey
Unwrapping the Castelli Secret	Caitlin Crews
A Marriage Fit for a Sinner	Maya Blake
Larenzo's Christmas Baby	Kate Hewitt
His Lost-and-Found Bride	Scarlet Wilson
Housekeeper Under the Mistletoe	Cara Colter
Gift-Wrapped in Her Wedding Dress	Kandy Shepherd
The Prince's Christmas Vow	Jennifer Faye

HISTORICAL

His Housekeeper's Christmas Wish	Louise Allen
Temptation of a Governess	Sarah Mallory
The Demure Miss Manning	Amanda McCabe
Enticing Benedict Cole	Eliza Redgold
In the King's Service	Margaret Moore

MEDICAL

Falling at the Surgeon's Feet	Lucy Ryder
One Night in New York	Amy Ruttan
Daredevil, Doctor...Husband?	Alison Roberts
The Doctor She'd Never Forget	Annie Claydon
Reunited...in Paris!	Sue MacKay
French Fling to Forever	Karin Baine

MILLS & BOON®
Hardback – April 2016

ROMANCE

MILLS & BOON®
Large Print – April 2016

ROMANCE

The Price of His Redemption	Carol Marinelli
Back in the Brazilian's Bed	Susan Stephens
The Innocent's Sinful Craving	Sara Craven
Brunetti's Secret Son	Maya Blake
Talos Claims His Virgin	Michelle Smart
Destined for the Desert King	Kate Walker
Ravensdale's Defiant Captive	Melanie Milburne
The Best Man & The Wedding Planner	Teresa Carpenter
Proposal at the Winter Ball	Jessica Gilmore
Bodyguard...to Bridegroom?	Nikki Logan
Christmas Kisses with Her Boss	Nina Milne

HISTORICAL

His Christmas Countess	Louise Allen
The Captain's Christmas Bride	Annie Burrows
Lord Lansbury's Christmas Wedding	Helen Dickson
Warrior of Fire	Michelle Willingham
Lady Rowena's Ruin	Carol Townend

MEDICAL

The Baby of Their Dreams	Carol Marinelli
Falling for Her Reluctant Sheikh	Amalie Berlin
Hot-Shot Doc, Secret Dad	Lynne Marshall
Father for Her Newborn Baby	Lynne Marshall
His Little Christmas Miracle	Emily Forbes
Safe in the Surgeon's Arms	Molly Evans

MILLS & BOON®

Why shop at millsandboon.co.uk?

Each year, thousands of romance readers find their perfect read at millsandboon.co.uk. That's because we're passionate about bringing you the very best romantic fiction. Here are some of the advantages of shopping at www.millsandboon.co.uk:

* **Get new books first**—you'll be able to buy your favourite books one month before they hit the shops

* **Get exclusive discounts**—you'll also be able to buy our specially created monthly collections, with up to 50% off the RRP

* **Find your favourite authors**—latest news, interviews and new releases for all your favourite authors and series on our website, plus ideas for what to try next

* **Join in**—once you've bought your favourite books, don't forget to register with us to rate, review and join in the discussions

Visit **www.millsandboon.co.uk**
for all this and more today!